James M. Cain Titles Available in Vintage

The Butterfly
—A story of incest in the mining country
of Appalachia

Double Indemnity
—An insurance salesman plans the
perfect murder

Love's Lovely Counterfeit
—A group of underworld figures struggles
to maintain its stranglehold on a Midwestern city

Mildred Pierce
—The story of a divorcee, her shiftless
husband and her monstrous daughter

The Postman Always Rings Twice
—A young vagrant and the bored wife
of a restaurant owner plan a murder, with
unexpected results

Serenade
—The chilling story of an opera singer,
a young conductor and a Mexican-Indian prostitute

THE
BUTTERFLY

James M. Cain

THE
BUTTERFLY

VINTAGE BOOKS
A Division of Random House, Inc.
New York

VINTAGE BOOKS EDITION, October 1979

Copyright 1946 and renewed 1974 by James M. Cain

All rights reserved under International and Pan-American Copyright Conventions. Published in the United States by Random House, Inc., New York, and in Canada by Random House of Canada Limited, Toronto. Originally published by Alfred A. Knopf, Inc., in 1947.

Library of Congress in Publication Data

Cain, James Mallahan, 1892-1977.
  The butterfly.
  Reprint of the 1947 ed. published by Knopf,
New York.
  I. Title.
PZ3.C11993Bu 1979   [PS3505.A31137]   813'.5'2
ISBN 0-394-75052-7   79-10814

Manufactured in the United States of America

Preface

THIS STORY goes back to 1922, when I was much under the spell of the Big Sandy country and anxious to make it the locale of a novel that would deal with its mine wars and utilize its "beautiful bleak ugliness," as I called it at the time, as setting. I went down there, worked in its mines, studied, trudged, and crammed, but when I came back was unequal to the novel; indeed, it was another ten years before it entered my mind again that I might be able to write a novel, for I had at least learned it is no easy trick, despite a large body of opinion to the contrary. But then I did write a novel, and the earlier idea began recurring to me—not the part about labor, for reflection had long since convinced me that this theme, though it constantly attracts a certain type of intellectual, is really dead seed for a novelist—but the rocky, wooded countryside itself, together with the clear, cool creeks that purl through it, and its gentle, charming inhabitants, whose little hamlets quite often look as they must have looked in the time of Daniel Boone. And then one day, in California, I encountered a family from Kentucky, running a roadside sandwich place. Certain reticences about a charming little boy they had led me to suspect he was the reason for the hegira from Harlan County, and the idea for a story began to take shape in my mind. The peculiarities of a birthmark possessed by one branch of my family helped quite a lot, and presently I had something fairly definite: a girl's disgrace, in a mountain village, which causes a family to make the grand trek to California, this trek being the main theme of the tale; the bitter, brooding unhappiness of all of them over California, with its bright, chirpy optimism, its sunshine, its up-to-date hustle; finally, a blazing afternoon, when the boy who started it all blows in, orders an egg malt, and finds himself staring into the murderous eyes of the girl's father.

Quite pleased with this fable, I drove to Huntington early in 1939, and cruised up and down both forks of the old familiar river, stopping at the old familiar places, picking up miners, visiting friends, noting changes, bringing myself down to date. Back in the West, I started to write, and the thing began to grow. And then Mr. Steinbeck published his *Grapes of Wrath*. Giving the project up was a wrench, but I had to, or thought I did, and presently was at work on something else. Bit by bit, traces of the abandoned book began appearing in other books: a beach restaurant in *Mildred Pierce*, divers recovering a body in *Love's Lovely Counterfeit*, a tortured soul, in *Past All Dishonor*, cornered and doomed, writing his apologia before his destiny catches up with him—though that had appeared in previous books, as it is occasionally forced on me by my first-personal method of narration.

But last summer, while *Past All Dishonor* was in the hands of the various experts who had to O.K. it before I could send it to the publisher, and I was having an interlude where all I could do was gnaw my fingernails, I happened to tell *The Butterfly* to a friend, who listened, reflected for a time, then looked at me peculiarly and said: "Now I understand the reason incest never gets written about, or almost never."

"Which is?"

"Because it's there, not in fact very often, but in spirit. Fathers are in love with their daughters. It's like what you said in *Serenade,* about there being five per cent of a homo in every man, no matter how masculine *he* imagines himself to be. But if a father happens to be also a writer and cooks up a story about incest, he's in mortal terror he'll be so convincing about it all his friends will tumble to the truth. You, though, you haven't any children, and I personally think you're a fool to give this book up."

"After the Joad family trip if I had a Tyler family trip I'd never live it down."

"Well, if you don't mind my saying so, I think that Tyler family trip is just dull, and all that California stuff so phony you'd throw it out yourself after you'd worked on it awhile—a wonderful, hot conflict between your description of the look in their eyes and your description of the scenery. That story is the story of a man's love for his own daughter, and the more it stays right up that mountain creek where it belongs and where you can believe it, the more it's going to be good. And look what you're throwing away for the damned California sunlight. That abandoned mine you told me about just makes my hair stand on end, and it's absolutely in harmony with that fellow's disintegration. What does California give you that compares with it? California's wholesome, and maybe it's O.K., but not for this. You go to it, and pretty soon you'll have a book."

So I started to work and it began to come, slowly at first, but presently at a better rate. I had to suspend for the *Past All Dishonor* changes, but soon was back on it, and at last, after the usual interminable rewrite, it was done. Re-reading it, now the final proofs are in, I like it better than I usually like my work, and yet I have an impulse to account for it; for most people associate me with the West, and forget, or possibly don't know, that I had a newspaper career of some length in the East before I came to California. Also, the many fictions published about me recently bring me to the realization I must relax the positivist attitude I carried over from newspaper work and be less reticent about myself. In an editorial room we like the positive article, not the negative; we hate rebuttals, and even when compelled to make corrections as to fact, commonly do so as briefly as possible. Thus, when false though possibly plausible assumptions began to be printed about me, I let them pass, for as a polemist I had acquired a fairly thick hide, and the capacity to let small things bounce off it without getting unduly concerned. But when these assumptions are repeated and I still don't deny them, I have only myself to blame if they become accepted as fact, and if elaborate deductions, some of them not so negligible, begin to be made from them. This may be an appropriate place, then, to discuss some of them, and perhaps get them discarded in favor of the truth.

I belong to no school, hard-boiled or otherwise, and I believe these so-called schools exist mainly in the imagination of critics, and have little correspondence in reality anywhere else. Young writers often imitate some older writer that they fancy, as for example I did when I used to exchange with my brother *You Know Me Al* letters, except that instead of baseball players we had the sergeants of 1918. We gave wonderful imitations of Lardner, and some traces of them, for any who care to look, can be seen in my book *Our Government,* the first sketch of which was written for the *American Mercury* in 1924. Yet if he can write a book at all, a writer cannot do it by peeping over his shoulder at somebody else, any more than a woman can have a baby by watching some other woman have one. It is a genital process, and all of its stages are intra-abdominal; it is sealed off in such fashion that outside "influences" are almost impossible. Schools don't help the novelist, but they do help the critic; using as mucilage the simplifications that the school hypothesis affords him, he can paste labels wherever convenience is served by pasting labels, and although I have read less than twenty pages of Mr. Dashiell Hammett in my whole life, Mr. Clifton Fadiman can refer to my hammett-and-tongs style and make things easy for himself. If then, I may make a plea on behalf of all writers of fiction, I say to these strange surrogates for God, with their illusion of "critical judgment" and their conviction of the definitive verity of their wackiest brainstorm: You're really being a little naïve, you know. We don't do it that way. We don't say to ourselves that some lucky fellow did it a certain way, so we'll do it that way too, and cut in on the sugar. We have to do it our own way, each for himself, or there isn't any sugar.

I owe no debt, beyond the pleasure his books have given me, to Mr. Ernest Hemingway, though if I did I think I should admit it, as I have admitted various other debts, mainly in the realm of theory, that were real and important, and still are. Just what it is I am supposed to have got from him I have never quite made out, though I am sure it can hardly be in the realm of content, for it would be hard to imagine two men, in this respect, more dissimilar. He writes of God's eternal mayhem against Man, a theme he works into great, classic cathedrals, but one I should be helpless to make use of. I, so far as I can sense the pattern of my mind, write of the wish that comes true, for some reason a terrifying concept, at least to my imagination. Of course, the wish must really have terror in it; just wanting a drink wouldn't quite be enough. I think my stories have some quality of the opening of a forbidden box, and that it is this, rather than violence, sex, or any of the things usually cited by way of explanation, that gives them the drive so often noted. Their appeal is first to the mind, and the reader is carried along as much by his own realization that the characters cannot have this particular wish and survive, and his curiosity to see what happens to them, as by the effect on him of incident, dialogue, or character. Thus, if I do any glancing, it is toward Pandora, the first woman, a conceit that pleases me, somehow, and often helps my thinking.

Nor do I see any similarity in manner, beyond the circumstance that each of us has an excellent ear, and each of us shudders at the least hint of the highfalutin, the pompous, or the literary. We have people talk as they do talk, and as some of them are of a low station in life, no doubt they often say things in a similar way. But here again the systems are different. He uses four-

letter words (that is, those dealing with bodily func-
tion); I have never written one. We each pass up
a great deal of what our ear brings us, particularly
as to pronunciation, which I never indicate, unless
the character is a foreigner and I have to give his
dialect, or a simplified version of it, else have him
pale and colorless. We are quite exact about the conventions we offer the reader, and accept Mark Twain's
dictum that it must be made clear, in first-personal nar-
rative, whether the character is writing or talking, all
small points being adjusted to conform. We each cut
down to a minimum the *he-saids* and *she-replied-
laughinglys*, though I carry this somewhat further than
he does, for I use the minimum number it is possible to
use and be clear, as a rule permitting myself only a *he-
said* to begin a patch of dialogue, with no others in between. For, when I started my *Postman Always Rings
Twice, he says* and *she says* seemed to be Chambers's
limit in this direction, which looked a bit monotonous.
And then I thought: Well, why all this *saying?* With
quotes around it, would they be gargling it? And so, if
I may make a plea to my fellow fiction-writers, I
should like to say: It is about time this convention,
this dreary flub-dub that lies within the talent of any
magazine secretary, was dropped overboard and forgotten. If Jake is to warn Harold, "an ominous glint
appearing in his eye," it would be a great deal smoother
and more entertaining to the reader, though I grant
you nothing like so easy, to slip a little, not too much of
course, but just the right subtle amount, of ominous
glint in the speech.

I grant, of course, that even such resemblances between Mr. Hemingway and myself do make for a certain leanness in each of us, as a result of all this skin-

ning out of literary blubber, and might be taken, by those accustomed to thinking in terms of schools, as evidence I had in some part walked in his footsteps. Unfortunately for this theory, however, although I didn't write my first novel until 1933, when he was ten years on his way as a novelist, I am actually six years and twenty-one days older than he is, and had done a mountain of writing, in newspapers and magazines, including dialogue sketches, short stories, and one performed play, before he appeared on the scene at all. My short story *Pastorale,* which you are probably encountering in current reprint, was written in 1927, though I first read him when *Men Without Women* appeared in 1928. Yet the style is pretty much my style today. Before leaving the subject, I may say that although for convenience of expression I have thrown what appears to be a very chummy "we" around his neck, I intend no familiarity and claim no equality. This, as I well know, is a Matterhorn of literature, while my small morality tale is at best a foothill. But small though it be, it is as good as I know how to make it, and I take some satisfaction in the fact that it is made well enough to reap some of the rewards mainly reserved for the small fable: It translates, so that it is known all over the world; its point is easily remembered, so that it passes easily from mouth to mouth and so lives on from year to year; I don't lack for at least as much recognition as I deserve, which is a fortunate situation to be in. But it does strike me as a very odd notion that in setting out to make it good I would do the one thing certain to make it bad.

Except personally, with many engaged in it, I am not particularly close to the picture business, and have not been particularly successful in it. True, several of my

stories have made legendary successes when adapted
for films, and when I choose I can usually obtain em-
ployment at reasonably good wages. I have learned a
great deal from pictures, mainly technical things. Yet
in the four years or more than I have actually spent on
picture lots, I have accumulated but three fractional
script credits. Picture people like to have me working
for them, they find me useful in solving difficult prob-
lems in their stories, they usually feel I earned my pay.
But they don't do my scripts. My novels, yes, after other
writers have worked them over. But not the copy I turn
out in their employ; apparently it hasn't the right flavor.
Why, I don't know and they don't, for as I have indicated, many of them are friends, and we discuss the
riddle freely. Moving pictures simply do not excite me
intellectually, or æsthetically, or in whatever way one
has to get excited to put exciting stuff on paper. I know
their technique as exhaustively as anybody knows it,
I study it, but I don't feel it. Nor have I ever, with one
exception, written a novel with them in mind, or with
any expectation of pleasing them. The exception was
Love's Lovely Counterfeit, which I thought, and still
think, is a slick plot for a movie, and I executed it well
enough. It didn't sell and is still for sale, if you happen
to want a good novel, only slightly marked down. All
my other novels had censor trouble, and I knew they
would have censor trouble while I was writing them,
yet I never toned one of them down, or made the least
change to court the studios' favor. In *Past All Dishonor,*
for at least four versions, the girl was not of the oldest
profession; she was the niece of the lady who ran the
brothel, and for four versions the story laid an egg.
I then had to admit to myself that it had point only
when she was a straight piece of trade goods. Putting

the red light over the door, I knew, would cost me a picture sale, and so far it has; it is in there just the same, and it made all the difference in the world with the book.

To have it asserted, then, by Eastern critics, that I had been "eaten alive by pictures," as one of them put it; that I had done all my research in projection rooms, and that this story was simply the preliminary design for a movie, was a most startling experience. It was said there were anachronisms in the speech, though none were specified, and that there were various other faults, due to the inadequacy of my researches. Well, I do my researches as other novelists do, so far as I know their habits: wherever I have to do them, in field or library or newspaper file, to get what I need for my story. In the case of *Past All Dishonor,* I did them in the Huntington, Los Angeles, Sacramento, Reno, and Virginia City libraries; in the *Official Record of the War of the Rebellion,* as published by the War Department, I having a set of my own, and in various directories, histories, newspapers, and diaries of the 1860's. For accuracy of speech I read hundreds of pages from the stenographic reports of witnesses before committees of Congress at the time, and as an additional check I re-read the writings of U. S. Grant, not the Memoirs, whose authenticity in spots is open to doubt, but his letters, and especially the long report in Part 1 of Vol. XXXIV of the *Official Record,* which was unquestionably written by him, in early middle age, less than two years after the time of my book. This as a sort of check, to make sure the terse, short-cadenced style I had in mind for Roger Duval had justification in the writings of the time. Grant, of course, seems as modern as Eisenhower; indeed, on the basis of all this reading, I con-

cluded that any notion the 1860's were noted for peculiarities of speech, or that quaint dialogue, such as some
of these critics seemed to think indicated, should be
used, was simply silly. Those people talked as we
talk now. Some words they used differently. They
said *planished* where we would say *burnished;* they
said *recruit* where we say *recuperate;* they *amused* the
enemy, where we would *divert* him. In general, however, they spoke in a wholly modern way, and I thought
it would be delightful for a modern reader to have
the lights turned up on a world he possibly had no
idea had ever existed. That my integrity would be
doubted, that it would be assumed that I got all
this from picture sets, I confess astonished me. The
Western reviewers, some of them specialists in the
Nevada of the silver boom, were most respectful to my
labors, as well as enthusiastic about the results; they
got the point of what I was trying to do, and several of
them called special attention to the circumstances that
here at last were miners who actually mined, instead
of standing around as extras in a saloon scene, and not
only mined, but had a grievous lot of trouble about it,
and formed unions, and ate, drank, and slept as miners
did eat, drink, and sleep at that time and in that place.
I was completely bewildered, I must confess, at the pat
statement of the New York critics, but I can't let them
pass uncorrected, which is the reason I ask your indul-
gence for this visit to the words-of-one-syllable department.

To revert, then, to Jess Tyler, the Big Sandy, and the
mine: The river empties into the Ohio not far from
Huntington, W. Va., and a few miles from its mouth
divides into two forks: the Levisa, which flows through
eastern Kentucky, and the Tug, which, with the Big

Sandy itself, forms the boundary between Kentucky and West Virginia. To the towns I have given fictitious names, but they are really factitious, a blend of characteristics, in so far as their characteristics are deemed of interest, from both sides of the river. Yes, I have actually mined coal, and distilled liquor, as well as seen a girl in a pink dress, and seen her take it off. I am 54 years old, weigh 220 pounds, and look like the chief dispatcher of a long-distance hauling concern. I am a registered Democrat. I drink.

James M. Cain

Los Angeles, Calif.
August 6, 1946

THE
BUTTERFLY

I

SHE WAS SITTING on the stoop when I came in from the fields, her suitcase beside her and one foot on the other knee, where she was shaking a shoe out that seemed to have sand in it. When she saw me she laughed, and I felt my face get hot, that she had caught me looking at her, and I hightailed it to the barn as fast as I could go. While I milked I watched, and saw her get up and walk all around, looking at my trees and my corn and my cabin, then go over to the creek and look at that and pitch a stone in. She was nineteen or twenty, kind of a medium size, with light hair, blue eyes, and a pretty shape. Her clothes were better than most mountain girls have, even if they were dusty, like she had walked up from the state road, where the bus ran. But if she was lost and asking her way, why didn't she say something and get it over with? And if she wasn't, why was she carrying a suitcase? When I was through milking, it was nearly dark, and I picked up my pails, came out of the barn, and walked over. "How do you do, miss?"

"Oh, hello."

"Is there something you want?"

"How can I tell till I know what you've got?"

She laughed, and I felt my face hot again, because from how she sounded and how she looked, she could have meant a whole lot more than she said. "Miss, I think there's a mistake. I think you're looking for somebody else's place, not mine."

"I'm looking for you."

"You never seen me before, so how do you know?"

"Maybe I saw your picture."

"Maybe you know my name?"

"Sure I know it. You're Jess Tyler."

". . . I asked you once, what do you want?"

"I told you once, how can I tell? . . . If you invited me in now, and told me to look around a little bit, why then I might pick something out."

"I don't like people making fun."

"Maybe I'm not."

She went to the pump, picked up the cup, and came back to where I had set down the milk. "I see one thing I want, right away."

"That milk's fresh, it's not cold."

"I like it warm, with foam on it."

She dipped up a cup, tasted it, then opened her mouth and poured it in. She gulped fast, but not fast enough, and a little ran out. "If somebody stuck their tongue out, they could stop that tickle on my chin."

I wiped with the back of my hand, and her eyes got a funny look in them, like I was pretty slow.

"Will you kindly tell your business?"

"Can't you take a hint? For one thing, it's supper

time, and I kind of feel like I could put away a little food."

"I never sent anybody away hungry."

"That's what I heard."

"Who from?"

"Don't you know?"

"No, I don't."

"Look who's raring up."

My cabin is log, but it's better than most, because it's always been in my family, and we're not trash like a lot of them around here. Some of the furniture goes back a hundred years, as you can tell from the dates carved on the chairs, but the plaster, whitewash, and underpinning I did myself, and some of the stuff I got when the coal camp broke up and people left things behind, specially the super, that give me four rag rugs. While I was cooking supper she went all over the front room and looked at everything in it, the pictures, settles by the fireplace, andirons, chairs, and knitted table covers, then got on her knees and felt the floor, because it's pine and gets scoured with sand every week, so it's white as snow and soft as silk. Then she did the same for the back room. Coming into the lean-to, where I was at the stove, she stopped and sniffed what I was cooking, and from the way her nose turned up I had her figured out, or thought I had. "Anyway, you're a Morgan."

"What makes you think that?"

"You favor them. They all look alike."

"The way you say it, it's nothing to be proud of."

"I wasn't saying any special way."

"Still, I guess no man likes his wife's family."

"He might, if he liked his wife."

"Didn't you like Belle?"

"Once, I loved her."

"And what then?"

"She killed it."

"How did she do that?"

"I don't want to talk about it."

"Did other men have something to do with it?"

"I don't say they didn't."

"And you put her out?"

"I never put her out. She left me."

"That was after the mine closed down?"

"It was after the mine closed down, and after the camp broke up. The seam feathered out to nothing, from a seven-foot seam of the finest steam coal in all this section, to just a six-inch layer that couldn't be worked. And for a year twenty or thirty of us drove tunnels in the rock, where they were hoping it would thicken up again, and we even put down a shaft, so if there was a jag in the seam we'd know it. We never found anything, but all during that time people were moving out, and she said them empty shacks got on her nerves. Then they backed up the trucks and took the shacks away, down to their No. 5 mine near Carbon City. Then they took the church and the store and the tipple and the railroad and everything away, so there was nothing there to get on your nerves. And then she moved out."

"Maybe she liked people."

"Maybe she liked a lot of things."

"You sound awful bitter."

"I told you once I don't want to talk about it."

"You ever see her anymore?"

"No, never."

"Or the children?"

"Not since she took them away."

"You ever want to?"

"Sometimes I think of them. Specially little Kady. Jane, she took after my grandmother, and had the same stony disposition. But Kady was cute."

"You know where they are?"

"Yes, I know."

We had hominy and chicken, that I had killed the day before and put in the well for the preacher, and after we ate she helped me wash up and it only took a little while. Then she wanted to see where the mine had been and the camp, so we took a walk in the moonlight and I showed her how it was laid out. Then we came back to my place and I showed her my corn- fields and hog pens and stable and barn, and explained to her how I had been just over the line from the com- pany land, so I never had to pay them rent when I worked in the mine, and I could make a little extra selling pop and stuff to the men, because I did it cheaper than the company store.

"Did you buy their land when the camp was taken away?"

"No, I didn't."

"That your corn growing on it?"

"I don't say it's not."

"You rent that field?"

"It might be I just plant it."

"You mean they like you?"

"Once a year they come out here and warn me to get off and stay off. Something about the law, I forget what. They can't admit I got a right there, I guess that's it."

"And what do you do?"

"I get off and stay off. One hour."

"You mean they just let you use that land?"

"I accommodate them a little bit. When they were first moving out, and all that machinery was up there in the tipple, I watched it for them. Things were kind of lively around here in those days, what with the union moving in and all, and sometimes dynamite got left in dangerous places, with the caps and stuff all ready to go off. Then later, if a rock got washed down, so it might fall on somebody and they'd be sued, I moved it for them or let them know. They treat me all right."

"I should say they do."

Under my apple trees she hooked little fingers with me. "Miss, you can stop doing things like that."

"Mister, why?"

"How old do you think I am?"

"I know how old you are. You're forty-two."

"Well, to you forty-two may look old, but to me it don't feel old. You don't watch out, something might happen to you."

"Not unless I want it to."

"If your name is Morgan, you would want it to."

"Even with you?"

"If he's a relation, that just makes it better."

"And if your name is Tyler, you wait at the head of the hollow till he goes by and then you shoot him in the back."

"I never shot anybody."

"We were talking about names, weren't we? Some people have got a name for one thing, some for something else."

"All I'm saying is, some things run in the blood."

"And all I'm saying is, there's blood and blood."

"And if it's there, you better fight it."

"What good does that do you?"

"If you don't know, nobody can't teach you."

"Maybe I already did some fighting. Maybe it didn't get me anything. Maybe I'm tired of fighting. Maybe I feel like cutting loose. Maybe I just want to be bad."

"That's no way to talk."

"It's one way."

When we got back to the cabin I told her she had to go, to get her things and I'd run her down to wherever she wanted to go, in the little Ford truck I use for hauling stuff. She went in the back room where her suitcase was, and was gone quite a while. When she came back she had taken off her clothes and put on a nightgown, wrapper and slippers. I tried to tell her to get dressed again, but nothing would come out of my mouth. She sat down beside me and put her head on my shoulder.

"Don't make me go."

"You got to."

"I couldn't stand it."

All of a sudden she broke out crying, and hung on to me, and talked all kind of wild stuff about what she'd been through, and how I had to help her out. Then after she quieted down a little she said: "Don't you know who I am?"

"I told you three times, no."

"I'm Kady."

". . . Who?"

"Your little girl. The one you like."

If I could write it down in this old ledger I'm using that I took her in my arms and told her to stay because she was my child, and could have anything from me she needed, I would do it, because on what happened later it would look like I never meant anything

like that at the start, and like I got into it without
really knowing what I was doing. But it wouldn't be
true. I took her in my arms, and told her to stay, and
fixed the back room for her, and took my own blankets
to the stable, where there's a bunk I can sleep in. But
all the time my heart was pounding at the way she made
me feel, and all the time I could see she knew how she
made me feel, and didn't care.

2

"WHAT WAS IT that happened to you?"

"What is it ever?"

"You mean a man?"

"If you could call it a man."

"And what did he do to you?"

"He left me."

"And what else?"

"That's all."

It was Sunday morning, and she was lying on the stoop in the sun, still in the pink gingham dress she had put on to help me with the feeding. I mumbled how sorry I was, and switched off to Blount, where Belle was running a boarding house for miners in the Llewelyn No. 3. Then all of a sudden she changed her mind, and did want to talk. "That's not all. There's a lot more to it than that. I didn't have much to say when you were talking about Morgans, did I? I know about that. I was twelve I guess when I woke up to a

few things that were going on. Jane, she knew about
them before I did, and we talked about it a lot, and
kept saying we would never be like that. And we decided the whole trouble, when you see something like
that, is how ignorant people are, like Belle not even
being able to read. And then we made up our minds
we were taking the bus every day and going to high
school. And that was when Belle got sick."

"Her sickness all comes out of a bottle."

"This was lung trouble."

"You mean she's really got lung trouble?"

"The doctor said if she was careful she'd get along,
but she couldn't work hard—so one of us had to run
the place. So Jane said it would be her."

"She sounds nice."

"She's just wonderful."

"She still favor me?"

"Yes, and we talked about you a lot, and it was on
account of you we wanted to go to school, because we
knew you read and wrote and went to church. So she
studied my books at home. Then when I graduated I
led the class, and at Blount last year they gave me a
job, teaching the second grade. I mean, little kids. It
caused a lot of talk that a miner's girl should teach
school, and there was a piece in the paper about it."

"Well, I'm proud of it."

"So was I."

She lay there looking at the creek for quite a while,
and I said nothing, because if she didn't want to tell
me about it I didn't want to make her. But she started
up again. "And then he came along."

"Who was he?"

"Wash Blount."

"He belong to the coal family?"

"His father owns Llewelyn. And because he used to be a miner, he thinks a miner's girl isn't good enough for his boy, and wants Wash to marry in a rich family, like the girl did, that lives in Philadelphia. So he kept after Wash. And at Easter he left me."

I said she'd get over it, and a couple more things, but then her face began to twist, and tears ran down her face, and she almost screamed the next thing she said. "And that's not all. In May they made me quit the school. Because they could see what I didn't know, what I wouldn't believe even when they told me, because I hadn't been a Morgan, only loving him in the most beautiful way. But it was true just the same. A month ago, in July, they took me to the hospital and I had a baby—a boy."

"Didn't that make you happy?"

"I hate it."

I asked her a few questions, and she told how Old Man Blount had paid the hospital bill, and was giving Belle an allowance, for the baby's board. Then she broke out: "To hell with it, and to hell with all this you've been telling me, about being good, and always doing the right thing. I was good, and look what it got me."

"No, you were bad."

"I wasn't. I loved him."

"If he loved you, he'd have married you."

"And who are you, to be having so much to say? You were good too, and it got you just what it got me. Didn't you know what Belle was doing to you? Didn't you know she was two-timing you with Moke?"

"He still around?"

"Him and his banjo."

Moke, I guess, had made me more trouble than anybody on earth, and even now I couldn't hear his name without a sick feeling in the stomach. He was a little man that lived in Tulip, which is not a town at all, but just some houses up the hollow from the church. His place was made of logs and mud, and he never did a day's work in his life that anybody hear tell of. But he had a banjo. Saturday afternoons, he played in at the company store and passed the hat around, and the rest of the time he hung around my place and played it. Belle said it was good for the pop drinking, but all I could see it might be good for was to hit him back of the ear with it, and then listen which made the hollower sound, it or his head. I got so I hated it and hated him. And then one day I knew what was going on. And then next day they were gone. Kady must have seen, from the look on my face, what I felt, because she said: "Nice, how they've treated you and me."

"That's in the past."

"I want to be bad."

"I'm taking you to church."

But all during the preaching she kept looking out the window at the mountainside, and I don't think she heard a word that was said. And later, when we shook hands with Mr. Rivers and those people from Tulip, she tried to be friendly, but she didn't know one from another even after I spoke their names. And some of them noticed it. I could see Ed Blue look at her with those little pig eyes he's got, and I didn't care for Ed Blue, and had even less use for him after what happened later, but I didn't want him talking around. Some of those people remembered her when she was a little thing, and wanted to like her, and giving him something to talk about wasn't helping any.

For apple-harvest, corn-husking, and hog-killing, I always got in two fellows from the head of the creek, and she fed us all three, and did a lot of things that had to be done, like running into Carbon City in the truck for something we needed, or staying up with me until almost daylight the night we boiled the scrapple. But when it got cold, and things slacked off a bit, and Jack and Mellie went home, she began sitting around all the time, looking at the floor and not saying anything. And then one night, after I'd been shelling corn all day, she asked what I did with it. "Feed it to the stock, mostly."

"Two mules, six hogs, two cows, and a few chickens eat up all that grain? My, they got big appetites. I never heard of animals as hungry as that."

"Some of it I sell."

"For how much?"

"Whatever they pay. This year, a dollar ten."

"That all you get?"

"It's according's according. Now you can sell it. But I've seen the time, and not so long ago, when you couldn't even give it away, and a dollar ten was a fortune."

"Bushel of corn's worth more than that."

"Who'll pay you more?"

"Café, maybe."

"Kady, what are you getting at?"

"You meal it and mash and just run it off once. You can get five dollars a gallon for it while it's still warm. You take a little trouble with it, you can get more. Put it away in barrels a couple of months you can get ten."

"People quit that when Prohibition went out."

"But they're starting up again, now the places can't get liquor. The mountain stuff goes in city bottles, and money is paid for it."

"Where'd you learn so much about this?"

"In Carbon, maybe I've been doing more than bringing back boxes for those apples of yours. Maybe I've found friends. Maybe they've told me how to get plenty of money quick."

"Did they tell you it's against the law?"

"Lot of things are against the law."

"And I don't do them."

"I want money."

"What for?"

"Clothes."

"Aren't those clothes pretty?"

"They look all right in a church on a mountain, but in Carbon they're pretty sick. I told you, I've been a sucker too long, and I'm going to step out."

"A church is better for you than a town."

"But not so much fun."

I shelled corn, and did no mealing or mashing. And one day she went off after breakfast and didn't come home till ten o'clock at night.

"Where have you been?"

"Getting me a job."

"What kind of a job?"

"Serving drinks."

"Where?"

"In a café."

"That's no decent job for a girl. And specially it's no job for a girl that has an education and can teach school."

"It pays better. And it is better."

"How do you figure that out?"

"Because if I feel like having a baby or something, they'd let me stay and not kick me out and after I had the baby they'd let me come back and be nice to it and be nice to me."

"What do you mean, feel like having a baby?"

"With the right fellow, it might be nice."

"Quit talking like that!"

She pulled off her hat, threw her hair around, and went to bed. It went on like that for quite a while, maybe two or three months, she staying out till ten, eleven, or twelve o'clock, us having fights, and me going crazy, specially when she began bringing home clothes that she bought, the way she told it with the tip money. But they must have been awfully big tips. And then came the night that she didn't come home at all, and that I didn't go to bed at all. I went down to meet the last bus, and when she wasn't on it I drove to Carbon City and looked everywhere. She was nowhere that I went to. I came back, lay on the bed, did my morning work, and then I knew what I was going to do.

That afternoon I saddled a mule and rode up a trail that ran up the mountain to a shack that the super had built when he was young and used to shoot. It was all dust and there was no furniture in it and it hadn't been used for a long time, but out back was what I was looking for. It was the old hot-water heater, with a coil inside, and the hundred-gallon tank, on a platform outside, that he had put in so him and his friends could have a bath any time they wanted.

"God but I'm glad you're back."

"Well look who's excited."

"I was afraid you weren't coming."

"We had to open a lot of cases, and we didn't get done until late and I missed the last bus. I stayed with a girl that works there."

My arms wouldn't let go of her, and we held hands while she ate the supper I had saved for her, and I was so happy a lump kept coming in my throat. And then when we were sitting in front of the fire I said: "That idea you had, remember?"

"About the corn?"

"Suppose I said yes. Would you quit this work you're doing, and stay out here and help me with it?"

"What's changed you?"

"I can't stand it when you're gone."

"Is it fifty-fifty?"

"Anything."

"Shake."

3

THE MINE, which was where I figured to set up our plant, scared me so bad I almost lost my nerve and quit before we began. Except maybe for rats and dust and spiders, I had thought it would be the same as when they took the machinery away, but when we got up there we found some changes had taken place. The top, where the weight of the mountain was on it, had bulged down in a bunch of blisters, about like the blisters on paint, except that they were the size of a wagon wheel instead of the size of a quarter, and as thick as a concrete road instead of as thick as a piece of paper. Each blister had split into pieces, and a lot of the pieces had fallen down, with the rest of them hanging there ready to kill you if you happened to be underneath when they dropped. And the floor had pumpkined up in wavy bumps that about closed the opening in a lot of places. So in the main drift, where I had thought we'd haul stuff in and out on a mine car, and

pull it up and lower it down with a falls to the old road-
bed below, there were three feet of jagged slabs with
a trickle of water running over them, and the car track
all buried. When she saw what it was like she begged
me not to go inside, but I crawled in to have a look.
After a hundred feet I had to stop. Because in the first
swag was a pool of water at least six feet deep, and
overflowing to make the trickle that was running out
the drift mouth.

When I got out we talked it over, and I had cold feet.
But she kept saying a coal mine wasn't the only place,
and she was sulky and I could see she didn't mean to
give up. And then I happened to remember one of those
tunnels we had driven the year when they were trying
to find out if there was any more thick seam. It wasn't
like a mine tunnel, where they drive their drift into a
layer of coal, and there's rock top and rock floor, with
coal for the rib and no need of timber, except of course
in the rooms where they rob the coal and have to put in
posts as they go or the whole thing would cave in. This
tunnel was through shale, with sandstone top, and we
had timbered as we went with cribbing. It was a quarter
mile around the mountainside, at the top of a straight
cliff that dropped into the creek, and we went around
there. Sure enough, there it was, all dirty and damp and
dark, but with the timbers still holding and the track
still in place. I lit up and crawled in, and saw a string of
cars on the first siding, about two hundred feet in. They
weren't the heavy steel cars they used on motor trains,
but little ones, that we had pushed by hand. I kept on,
and found all entries open, even the ones that connected
with the worked-out part of the mine, though they were
full of slabs, like the main drift. And then at last I came
to what I'd been headed for since I first crawled in the

old drift mouth, which was the shaft that was sunk for ventilation, and because it would crosscut everything, and they could see if they had anything or not, and when they found out they hadn't, they quit.

"It's all there, everything, just like we want it, and specially the shaft. It's light enough down there to see what we're doing, we can set up scaffolds for our tubs, tanks, and kegs, so all our stuff will run downwards, and we won't have to pump. We even got our water just like we want it, because that pool in the swag, it comes from a spring that runs down one side of the shaft, and it's good sweet water, because I tasted it to make sure. We can trap it halfway up, and run it wherever we want. And nobody will find the top of that shaft, or see it from down on the road, or smell anything. And there won't be any smoke, because we'll use charcoal, and it don't make any. But how do we get anything up there?"

"You said a block and falls?"

"From the old railroad bed, not from the creek."

"Could we—use a boat?"

"Yeah, and we could put an ad in the paper."

"I guess it would look pretty funny."

"We could figure it out, maybe, why we got the only boat on the creek, but everybody from the state road to Tulip would ask us about it, and when you start something like this you can't have any asking."

We were climbing down, through the dogwood that was just coming out, and when we got to the water we crossed over the footbridge that led to my land, and began walking upstream. Then I noticed that the road and the cliff, from the way the stream narrowed at that place, weren't really so far apart. There was kind of a sandbar that made out from the bank where the road

was, but just the same, by using a long boom, anybody
on the cliff could throw a light line to somebody parked
on the road, and if the line was attached to the block,
it could be pulled across as it went down, and then when
whatever was going up was hooked on, the light line
would steady it, so it wouldn't smash against the cliff.
Then when the hoisting was finished, everything could
be pulled up out of sight, and put away till next time. I
explained it to her, and she got it, but began asking
questions about it. "My goodness, Jess, talk about a
boat, me parked in a truck across the road, blocking
traffic, while you pull stuff up with two or three pulleys
squeaking, that's not exactly secret."

"What traffic? We do it at night."

"That's right. Nobody's out at night."

"We don't make any new track or path to give us
away. You handle the truck and I handle the falls. If
we hear anything I pull up and you drive off, that's all."

"I love it."

"Now we're set, except for one thing."

"What's that?"

"The tank, from the shack. We can't haul that up. We
got to pack it by muleback, if I can ever figure some
kind of cradle to put it in. We take it to the shaft
mouth, then lower it down."

"Well, I bet we can haul it up."

"How do we get it through the tunnel?"

"Oh. Now I see."

"It's just not big enough."

So we went to work, and it split up about even, the
things I could do and she couldn't, and the things she
could do and I couldn't have made myself do in a hundred years. I'm no mechanic, but I'm handy with tools,

and all the stuff that had to be made and connected up, there was no trouble about it, except it took time and was a lot of work. Like I told her, the first thing was the hundred-gallon tank from the shack up the mountainside, but I got a light wagon up there, and when I started down with it there were a couple of places where I had to use planks, ropes, and chocks to work it along, but I had a lot less trouble with it than I expected, and got it to the shaft mouth in one day. Another day saw it lowered down inside, and I could go ahead with my scaffolds. For them I used lumber from the old loading platform of the railroad, and for pipe to connect everything up I used the water pipe of the old filling station. I kept steady at work, and it wasn't very long before I had one deck of tubs, covered over with lids, and one leading to the other, where I trapped the water from the spring, and connected it with my mash tubs, on the next deck, and my still, which was right on the ground. For my heating chamber I used the tank, and for the cooling system the old heater, with the coils reconnected so they ran down through cold water. I figured everything out pretty good, like the intake of cold water down at the bottom, the drain for hot water at the top, so once we got started it all worked almost automatic.

She attended to whatever had to be done in Carbon City, and that was plenty, but I couldn't have gone in there and had people look at me, and know from what I was buying what I was up to. She got the tubs we needed for the water, and for the mash, and the kegs for aging the liquor. Everything had to be small, on account of the tunnel, as I didn't want to drag any more stuff to the shaft mouth than I could help, but nothing gave us much trouble but the kegs. They were supposed to be charred, but I couldn't see that they were, so we had to char them. While I worked on my pipe, she'd fill them with chips and shavings, until they were almost full up to the one end I'd left open after slipping the hoops and taking out the head. When it was going good with the flame she'd roll it around with the hook end of the fire poker she'd brought up from the cabin, until all over the inside was what they call the "red layer." Then we'd souse water in it, and next day I'd put the head back in and tighten the hoops, and we had one more container ready. For all that stuff I gave her money, but it didn't cost as much as I had thought it would, because she got a lot of it second-hand, and beat them down when she could. But some things, I don't know where she could have bought them. For instance, the hydrometer she got, that you have to have to test the proof with, came in a long pasteboard box. And stamped on the box was "Property of Carbon City High School." I kept telling myself I had to ask her about it, but I never did.

After a long time, after staying up late mealing corn, making charcoal, and doing all kinds of things that had to be done, came the day when we warmed some water in the still and put down our first mash. And three days after that we made our first run. I felt nervous, because even if nobody could see us it was against the law and against all the principles I had. But it was pretty too, after you got going with it. On a little still you put in a toothpick, but on this one we used a skewer, a wooden pin that you dress meat with, that's sharp on one end and six or eight inches long. We stuck it in the end of the pipe, where the coil came out, and as the fire came up, there came this funny smell I had never smelled be-

fore but that I liked, and the pin began to get wet. Then
on the sharp end, that was outside, came a drop, like
the drop of a honeysuckle when you pull the cord
through to taste yourself some honey. It fell in the
fruit jar we had under it, and then pretty soon here
came another drop. Then the drops were falling one
after the other. Then they came together in a little
stream, the color of water, but clearer than any water
you ever saw. When the first jar was full, she poured it
in the tall glass that the hydrometer worked in, dropped
the gauge in, and took the proof.

"What does it say?"

"One seventy."

"Very good."

"My goodness, if it's that strong at the start we can
run it clear down to thirty and it'll still be one hundred
when we mix it for the keg."

"We'll run till it mixes one twenty-five."

"The more we get the more we've got."

"Maybe this is a case where the less you act like a
hog, the more you put on some fat. We can run it till
we got a lot and put it in the wood at a hundred. But
then it dries out and gets weaker, and if it's weak it
won't sell. And the weaker it is, the slower the charcoal
works on it. If we put it in strong, we got color, flavor,
and mellowness in a month, anyway enough to be a big
help when it's mixed with regular liquor. But at a hundred we could be a year and we'd get nothing they'd
pay us for. The longer we got to keep it, the more kegs
we got to buy, the longer we wait for our money."

"That money's what I want."

"Then watch it, it don't get too weak."

"Then anyway we can have music."

She had a little radio up there by then, and turned it

on, and I didn't mind, as it would be a long day, watching that stream off the end of the pin.

"And a drink."

"What?"

"What we making the stuff for?"

"You mean this?"

"Sure."

She climbed up, got a bottle of Coca-Cola out of the basin the spring ran into, and the tin cup we kept there. When she came down she poured from the jar to the cup, dumped some Coca-Cola in, and handed it to me.

"Taste it, it's good."

Now nobody could live their life in mountain country without learning plenty about whisky, but that was the first time I ever tasted it. It tasted like Coca-Cola at first, but then I began to feel good, and wanted another swallow. She had the cup by then, taking a swig, and then was when I knocked it out of her hand.

"There's to be no drinking in this."

"I'll have a drink if I want to."

"No, you won't."

"Will you kindly tell me why?"

"We got work to do for one thing. I get careless with this fire, so it's too hot, this whole thing could explode so easy you wouldn't believe it. And later, when it's dark, we've only just begun. We've got to lower this spent mash down, so we can feed it to the hogs and not have it all over the place, and we can't do that or anything if we're up here drunk. And we'll get drunk, if we take enough of it. They all do. I've seen them. And besides, it's wrong."

"You believe all you hear in church?"

"I believe what I feel."

"For God's sake."

Because by then I loved her so much I wanted to be weak, and do what she meant we should do, but my love made me strong too, so I knew I wouldn't do it. With liquor in me, though, I didn't know what I would do, or what she could make me do. "You heard me, Kady? That's one thing we don't do."

"I heard you."

4

AND THERE CAME the night when we drove into Carbon City with our first hundred quarts, packed in every bag and sack and poke I could find, and yet all you could hear was glass, rattling louder even than the truck. I thought I would die, and when she left me, after I parked by the railroad, everything from the chirp of crickets to the clank of yard signals just gave me the shivers. After a long time she was back, with a café man, and he had a flashlight, so I wanted to holler at him, and tell him to put it out. But we had it set that she'd do the talking, so I sat there and wiped off sweat. They talked along, and he put the light on a bottle for color, then did some tasting and handed it back. "It might not be so bad, sister, except it's all full of caramel."

"O.K. I'll take it up the street."

"Can't you taste it?"

"What would I be tasting it for? I made it, dumb-bell. That color's charcoal, that I burned in the keg myself, as anybody would know except maybe a jerk that hadn't seen good booze for so long he's forgot what it's like. But it's all right, and no hard feelings. I'll just take it where they know what it means to have some hundred ten proof in the house that makes blended stuff taste like something, and kick a little bit too."

"What do you mean, hundred ten proof?"

"Get your tester."

"Mine's broke."

"Then I brought one."

She got out the hydrometer and let him take a reading. "If you think that gauge is loaded, try a slug yourself."

He took a swig, while she stood there looking at him so sinful it made me sick to think she was any part of me. Then he took another, and you could see it take hold. "What are you asking for it?"

"Ten dollars a gallon."

"I'll give you four."

"Oh, I'm going up the street."

"No, wait a minute, let's talk."

They closed at six, and I ran them to the alley back of his place, where he went in and got the money and had the bottles carried in. Then she jumped in beside me.

"Come on, Jess, let's celebrate."

"What do you call celebrating?"

"Just going somewhere, having a good time."

"What was the idea, looking at him like that?"

"Well my goodness, I was selling him booze."

"What else were you selling him?"

"The way you talk."

We drove under a bridge, then came to a café called the White Horse and stopped. I had never been in a place like that, but I no sooner saw it than I knew it was the kind of place I'd been hearing about all my life, and that it was bad. The lights were low, and on one side was a bar, on the other side booths, and in the middle a place where couples were dancing to slow music that came out of a box at one end, with lights in it. The crowd no sooner saw Kady than they began to yell, and come to find out it was where she used to work. I didn't thank her when she said she'd brought her old man, and I didn't offer to shake anybody's hand. We sat down in a booth and I told the girl two Coca-Colas. "Make mine a rum coke."

"Two Coca-Colas."

"Listen, Jess, I want a drink."

"We're going home."

"If you don't like it here, you can go home, and I'll stay, and I'm quite sure somebody will take me in for the night."

So anything that meant she might leave me, that got me, and I shut up. But I was swelling up thick inside.

In the next booth was a girl and two men, that were mine guards from the way they talked, and when one of them and the girl left, the other one got up and asked Kady to dance. She went off with him, and they went to the music box, and their heads were together while they dropped in their nickel. Then they danced, and when the tune was almost over they danced by the box, stopped, and dropped more money in, at least a dozen nickels, one right after the other. Then when a tune stopped, it would be only a few seconds before another one started, but during that time they didn't stop dancing. They stood there, swinging to the music that wasn't playing any more, and then when it started again they'd go off. About the third tune, they made signs to the bartender, and he made them drinks that they picked up as they went around, and sipped, and left on the bar. About the tenth tune they were dancing with their faces up against each other, and had forgot their drink. Then they stopped and stood there whispering. Then she came over and picked up her handbag. "I won't be long, Jess."

"Where you going?"

"Just for a walk. Get a little air."

"You're coming home."

"Sure. Soon we'll go."

"We're going now."

The man walked over and stepped between us. "Listen, pop, take it easy why don't you?—so we don't have any trouble."

"Do you know who I am?"

"You're Kady's father, so she says."

"And I'm taking her home."

"Not unless she wants to go, pop. Now the way she tells me, she feels like taking a walk, and that's what we're going to do. So sit down. Don't get excited. Have yourself a drink, and when her and me get back you're taking her home. But not before."

He put on his hat, one of those black felts turned down on one side like a mountain gunman wears, and looked me in the eye. He was tall and thin, and I could have broke him in two, but that gun was what I kept thinking about. A mine guard is never without it, and he knows how to use it, and he will use it. I could feel the blood pounding in my neck, but I sat down. He turned to his booth and sat down.

While we were having that, she had said something to him about the ladies' room, and gone back there. I sat with my throat pounding heavier all the time, until a door back there opened, and she started walking up to his booth. I don't remember thinking anything about it. But when she was almost to him, I grabbed that booth partition, and pulled, and it crashed down, and there he was, sprawling at my feet. I was on him even before she screamed, and when that gun came out of his pocket, I had it. I brought it down on his head, he crumpled, I aimed, and pulled the trigger. But I had forgot the safety catch, and before I could snap it off, they grabbed me.

"This court, unless compelled, is not going to make a criminal out of a father defending the honor of a daughter. But it is not going to overlook, either, a breach of the peace that could have had the most serious consequences. Tyler, do you realize that if these witnesses hadn't prevented it, you would have killed a man, that you would now stand before me accused of the crime of murder, that it would be my unescapable duty to hold you for the grand jury, and that almost certainly you would in due time be found guilty, sentenced, and hanged?"

"Yes sir."

"Do you think that's right?"

"I guess I don't."

"How much money is in your pocket?"

"Fourteen dollars, sir."

"Then just to impress it on your mind that this is more than a passing matter, you can pay the clerk here a fine of ten dollars and costs for disorderly conduct— or perhaps you'd rather spend the next ten days in jail?"

"I'd rather pay, sir."

"Young woman, how old are you?"

"Nineteen, sir."

"Have you been drinking?"

"I—don't know, sir."

"What do you mean you don't know?"

"Well, I was drinking Coca-Cola, but you know how it is. Sometimes they put a little something in it, just for fun, but tonight I don't know if they did or not."

"Lean over here, so I can smell your breath. . . . How can you have the cheek to tell me you don't know if you've been drinking or not, when you're half shot, right now? Aren't you?"

"Yes, sir."

"Do you realize that I can hold you with no more evidence than that as a wayward minor, and have you committed to a school?"

"I didn't know it, sir."

"There are a great many things you don't seem to know, and my advice to you is that you turn over a new leaf, and do it now. I'm remanding you into the custody of your father, and on the first complaint from him, you're up for commitment. Do you understand that, Tyler? If there's any more trouble like what went on in there tonight, you don't grab a gun and start shooting. You come to me, and the proper steps will be taken."

"Yes, sir, I understand it."

"Next case."

Going home she was laughing at how funny it was, that he hadn't asked her how much money *she* had, because she still had every cent of the hundred and fifty dollars we had got for the liquor, but after we got home and got a fire going and ate something and drunk some coffee, I shut her up. "You want to go to that reform school?"

"You mean you'd send me?"

"If you don't shut up, I might."

"Can't I even laugh?"

"He was right."

Then we began to talk, and I tried to tell her how it scared me, that I had almost killed a man. "And you, don't it shame you, you were making up to two men tonight, within ten minutes of each other?"

"What's to be ashamed of?"

"It's blood."

"Listen, if I hear any more of this Morgan stuff—"

"I tell you, it's in-breeding. It's what we both got to be afraid of. It's in us, and we ought to be fighting it. And stead of that—"

"Yeah, tell me."

"We're not."

"Well say, that's terrible."

" 'Shining, shooting, and shivareeing their kin, that's what they say of people that live too long on one creek. I thought I was too good for that. But today, right up in that mine, I ran off five gallons of liquor that's against the law. This evening I almost killed a man."

"And tonight you'd like to have me."

"Stop talking like that!"

"What were you shooting him for?"

"You ought to know."

"You must be loving me plenty."

"I told you, quit that!"

"Have a drink with me?"

"No!"

"How about *you* going to reform school?"

5

ONE NIGHT WHEN I got through the run I took a walk
up the creek, and when I came to the church I kept on
up the hollow, and pretty soon sat down by a tree and
tried to think. We had had some trouble that day. Now
the money was coming in she kept buying clothes, blue
and yellow and green dresses, and red coats, and hats
with ribbons hanging down the side, and every night
we'd drive in town to the White Horse, and they
wouldn't serve her liquor any more but we'd have some
cokes, and then she'd dance and carry on with whoever
was there, and then I'd take her home. But in the day-
time she got sloppier and sloppier, and one day when
it got hot she took off her shoes. And this day she said
it was so hot by the still she couldn't stand it, and
slipped off her dress so she was in nothing but under-
wear and hardly any of that, and began dancing to the
radio, swaying with the music with one hand on her
hip and looking me in the eye. Well, in the first place,

in a coal mine it's the same temperature all the year round, and that little bit of fire I had in there, what with the ventilation we had, didn't make any difference at all. So we had an argument about it, and I made her put her clothes on and cut off the music. Then she said: "Jess, did it ever strike you funny, one thing about this place?"

"What's that?"

"If a woman was attacked in here, there's nothing at all she could do about it."

"Couldn't she bite? Or kick? Or scratch?"

"What good would it do her?"

"Might help quite a lot."

"Not if the man was at all strong. She could scream her head off, and not one person on earth would hear her. I've often thought about it."

"Funny, what some people got their mind on."

I made her get out of there and go down to the cabin and catch up on some of the work. But I was hanging on by my teeth by that time, and I was a lot nearer giving up the fight, and going along with her on whatever she felt like doing, even getting drunk, than I wanted her to know. That was when I took this walk up the creek, and past the church, and through Tulip, trying to get control of myself, and maybe pray a little, for some more strength.

And then, from up among the trees, I heard something that sounded like a wail. Then here it came again, closer. Then I could make out it was a man, calling somebody named Danny. And then all of a sudden a prickle went up my back, because I knew that voice, from the million times I had heard it at the company store and around the camp and in my own home. It was Moke, but he wasn't singing comical stuff to a banjo now. He was scared to death, and slobbering at the mouth as he called, and in between moaning and whispering to himself. He went stumbling along to his cabin, and I followed along after him, and watched while he stood in the door, a candle in his hand, and called some more. Then when he went inside I crept up and peeped through a chink in the logs. He was a little man, but I never saw him look so little as he looked now. He was sitting on the clay floor, in one corner, the banjo leaning against the wall beside him, his head on his arms, and shaking with sobs so bad you thought they were going to tear him apart.

I was shook up plenty myself, because if there was one person in this world I hated it was him, and after all Kady had said, and all I knew from before, I couldn't help wondering what he was doing here, and I knew it had to be something that meant me. So I could feel some connection when I came to my cabin, and from the back room I could hear a baby crying. I went inside, and at the sound of the door, a woman called to know if it was Kady. I said it was Kady's father. She came out then, and from the tall, thin shape she had, and the look of her face and color of her eyes, I knew she was a Tyler. "I think you're my girl Jane."

"And you're my father."

We shook hands, and I patted her hand, and then we sat down, and both of us wanted to give each other a kiss but were too bashful. "Can I call you Father?"

"I don't mind."

"I used to call you Pappy."

"You remember that?"

"I remember a lot, and how sweet you was to me, and how much I loved you, and how tall you was."

"Why not call me Jess?"

"Isn't that fresh?"

"Kady does, but of course she *is* fresh."

"It's so wonderful about her."

". . . What about her?"

"Everything."

She looked down at the floor, and you could see she was awful happy about something, and then she said: "You know about Danny?"

"Who's Danny?"

"Didn't she tell you?"

"Is that Danny in there crying?"

"He won't cry after he's fed. Kady took the truck and ran into town for a lot of things he's got to have, because all you've got here, that he can have, is milk. But she'll be back soon. And as soon as he gets a little something in his stomach he'll be sweeter than sugar."

"What's Moke got to do with him?"

"Have you seen Moke?"

I told her what had gone on in the hollow, and she doubled up her fists and said: "I hope I don't see him. I might kill him."

"Hey, hey, none of that kind of talk."

"Moke took Danny."

"First my wife, then my grandson."

"Say that again, Jess."

"He is, isn't he?"

"I wasn't sure you'd remember it."

"I don't forget much."

"What Moke did, and how today I caught up with him, that's part of what's so wonderful. Last week, on account of Kady being gone and my mother not much caring one way or the other, little Danny was mine, and it was heavenly, because maybe I'll never get married, but still I had one of my own. Then when I came home from the store one day he was gone, and Moke was gone, and I went almost crazy, but I knew it had to be Moke that took him, because he was so crazy about him."

"Moke loves somebody?"

"Oh, he gets lonely too. And there I was, fit to be tied. Because Kady, that was my whole life before, was gone I had no idea where, and now with Danny stolen it was more than I could stand. But my mother said if Moke took him, he had to have some place to bring him to, and he still had his shack up in the hollow, and maybe it was there. So she drew it out for me how to get there, and I took the bus over from Blount, and even before I got to it I could hear Danny laughing and Moke playing to him on the banjo. So I wasn't going to take any chance on a fight with Moke. Maybe he wouldn't let me have Danny, but then he'd know I was around, and might run off again, somewhere else. So he said something to Danny about a drink, but I noticed there was no well out back."

"He gets water from a neighbor."

"I thought he might, and right away he came out with a pail and started across the clearing. I went in and grabbed Danny and ran down the path, and when I got to the road I made a man with a wagon give me a ride, because he said he was going as far as the bus line. But then, as we passed this cabin, *who should I see but Kady out back, hanging out clothes!* Jess, I jumped down, and ran over to her, and I wasn't crazy any more, I was the happiest person on earth, because I had my two darlings back, my little baby, and my sister that I'd loved ever since I could remember."

"How does Kady feel about it?"

"She loves it."

I didn't love it, and if Kady did, that wasn't how she told it to me, the last time she had mentioned Danny. But when she came in with the stuff she'd bought, her eyes were like stars, and she went in the back room with Jane without even a hello to me. I sat there trying to tell myself it was all right, it was just what I'd been praying for. If she could love her child, and stop all this drinking and dancing and carrying on, it was the best thing all around, and I could get some peace from her, and not be teased into having thoughts about her that made me so ashamed I hated to own up to myself they were there. It didn't do me any good. If she'd had a child, and she hated it, that squared it up, and I didn't have to remember it. But if she didn't hate him, it was between me and her, and would be, always. I sat there, while out back Jane explained how to mix this and how to cook that, and pretty soon they began feeding the baby, and his crying stopped and Jane began talking to him and telling him how pretty he was, and all of a sudden Kady was sitting beside me and picking up my hand.

"Want to see my baby, Jess?"

"I guess not."

"He's a pretty baby."

"So I hear."

"And he's your grandson."

"I know."

"It would make me happy, Jess."

"It wouldn't me."

"Then if that's how you feel about it, I won't try to

change you. I'll take him away. There's a reason I can't go back to Blount just yet, but he and Jane and I can stay in a hotel at Carbon and you won't be bothered."

"I didn't ask you to leave."

"If my baby's not welcome, I'm not."

"You've changed a lot, that's all I can say."

"Didn't Jane tell you why?"

"Not that I know of."

"Didn't she tell you why Moke took him?"

"She said he was lonesome."

"He loved Danny, and specially after the way Belle began fighting with him, just before I left. He was crazy about him, and then when he found out he was to be taken away, he went off with him."

"Who was going to take him away?"

"Jane ran into Wash."

"The father?"

"Yes."

"Or it might be shorter just to say rat."

"He's no rat."

"He skipped like a rat."

"His father made him. And then, a week ago, Jane ran into him on the street, in Blount. And he asked about me, and Danny, and was friendly, and pretty soon Jane came right out with it and asked why he didn't marry me, and give his little boy a name, and stop being—"

"A rat."

"Anyway, Jess, what he said was wonderful."

"What was it he said?"

"He said he was always going to, soon as he was twenty-one, whether his family liked it or not. He's only twenty, Jess, one year older than I am. But now, he said they would give their consent too, before he was twenty-one. Because an awful thing happened to them. His sister, the one that married into the coal family in Philadelphia, had to have an operation, and now she can't have any children any more. And now they know if they're to have grandchildren, it's got to be through Wash. And now they feel different about Danny. And —so do I. I'm so ashamed how I treated him before."

"Well, it's all fine."

"Are you glad at all, Jess?"

"To me, a rat's a rat."

"Not even for my sake you don't feel glad?"

"I rather not say."

Tears came in her eyes and she sat there making little creases in her dress. It wasn't one of those she'd been buying, but a quiet little blue one, that made her look smaller and younger and sweeter. I said she should stay on till it suited her to go and I'd go to Carbon, but she said she'd go, and I hated it, the way I was acting, and yet I couldn't help how I felt. And then Jane was there, putting something in my lap, and looking up at me was the cutest little child I ever saw, all pink and soft and warm, with nothing on him but a clean white diaper. Kady reached over to take him, but I grabbed him and went over to one of the settles by the fire and sat there and held him close. And for a long time something kept stabbing into my heart, and I'd look at him and feel so glad he was partly mine that I wanted to sing. His diaper slipped down a little and I almost died when I saw a brown bug on his stomach, or what I thought was a brown bug, just below the navel. I reached for it with my fingers, but Jane laughed.

"That's his birthmark."

"I thought it was some kind of a moth."

"It's his butterfly."

"It almost scared me to death."

They went in the back room with him again, but I called Kady out. "I take it back, everything I said. He's so sweet I could eat him."

"But if you'd rather I went—"

"I couldn't stand it if you did."

"I can understand how you feel."

"But I don't! Not any more. It's all gone, the devilment that's been in me, and the onriness, and all what I've been thinking about. I want you to be happy. And if the boy wants to marry you, he's not any rat, and I want you to have him."

"I'm so glad, Jess."

"Me too."

"I want to be your little girl."

"And I want to be your pappy."

"Kiss me."

I kissed her, and she kissed me back, and it wasn't like those hot kisses we'd been having, but cool and sweet like the kiss Danny gave me just before they took him away.

6

WHY SHE COULDN'T GO to Blount right away she didn't
tell me till one day when all four of us were sitting out
under the trees and I spotted a big car coming up the
creek from the state road. Then she owned up she had
wired the boy, and yet she wasn't going back till he
came and got her. So she and Jane ran in the house
with Danny to get slicked up and in another minute
there he was, kind of a tall, dark boy in slacks and blue
shirt. He didn't put on any airs with me at all, but shook
hands quick, and went around the cabin looking at it,
and said it was just like the one his uncle had on Paint
Creek, where he used to spend part of every summer.
So then it turned out his father had got himself a mine,
but his family were mountain people, like us. So that
went with his bony look, and made me feel still better
about him. Then when Kady came out and he took her
in his arms, I had to begin fooling around with my shoe
for fear they'd see the tears in my eyes. Then when he

saw Danny for the first time in his life, in Jane's arms laughing and trying to talk as she brought him out, he went over and bent over and looked and bent down and called him old-timer and shook hands just like it was somebody he was being introduced to and could say something. Then he tried to brush off the butterfly, just like I had, and we all laughed and had some Coca-Cola and were friendly. But when they went in to get supper he said he'd have to leave for a little while. "If you're going back to town, I'll ride along with you. There's some things I ought to get."

"I'm going up the creek."

"There's nothing up the creek."

"There's a heel named Moke Blue."

"You know Moke?"

"I've seen him and I guess I've spoken to him, but I've never shaken his hand and until I got Kady's wire I never even thought about him. I'm thinking about him now, though. And I'm putting him in jail for kidnapping my boy."

"You're taking him in, yourself?"

"That's it, Jess."

"I'll go with you."

"You mean we'll do it together?"

"Soon as I get my rifle."

"I won't need it."

"How you know?"

"He's got no gun, I'm sure of it."

"He could get one, and anyway, all he'd have to do is holler and about eighteen brothers and in-laws and cousins would be there, and at least half of them have guns."

"If we bring a gun, Jess, I'll kill him."

"Maybe we better not."

We got in his car and rode up as far as the church, then got out and walked up the hollow to the end of the path, then followed the gully up to Moke's shack. Nobody was in it, and except for some beans in one corner that didn't prove much, there was no way to tell if anybody had been there for the last two or three days, or had just stepped out and would be right back, or was up the hollow or down the creek. But while we were whispering about it he held up his hand and I looked. Through a cornfield, just below us, a boy was moving on tiptoe, toward the woods on the other side of the gully.

"You know him, Jess?"

"Birdie Blue. He's Moke's cousin."

"He's gone to tip him."

"Then he'll be back, to keep watch."

"If we time him, we'll know how far he went."

He took out his watch, and we waited and I kept an eye on him, and the more I saw of him the better I liked him. He didn't talk, but kept staring at the place the boy had to cross on his way back, and he had that mountain look in his eye that said if it took a week he'd still be staring, but he'd do what he came for. In a half hour the boy showed, and then all of a sudden Wash got up.

"We're a pair of boneheads, Jess."

"What we done now?"

"The banjo's gone!"

"Well?"

"If he was in hell waiting to be fried he'd still have to pick the damned thing. Come on."

There was no window in the back of the shack, but there was a loose log, and we pushed it out and crawled through. Then we crept up the gully, keeping the shack between us and the boy, where he was squatting in the bushes, keeping watch on my hat, that we left in the doorway to keep him interested. It was around sundown, and the mosquitoes were beginning to get lively, but we kept from batting them somehow, and pretty soon we came to a place where Wash stopped and looked around, and whispered if there was any sounds in the neighborhood, we'd catch most of them here, because sound travels upward. And sure enough, there were all sorts of things you could hear, from the creek going over the stones near the church to people talking in cabins and birds warbling before going to sleep. And then he grabbed my arm, and we listened, and there was the sound of the banjo. He stood up, and turned first one way, then the other way, then covered one ear, then the other ear, and in a minute he knew where it was coming from, and we crept over there. And when we got there it was a little stone well, with a frame over it and an iron wheel, and Moke was sitting on the rim, his head lopped over on one side, the banjo across his belly, plunking out sad chords that weren't like the comical tunes he used to play, and looking so little he was more like some kind of a shriveled-up, gray-haired boy than what he was, a man. Wash crept around the well from behind him, grabbed him by the shirt collar, and jerked him over on his side, so he let out a little whimper. "What you doing to me? Wash, what are you doing here?"

"Didn't the boy tell you I was here?"

"How would he know? He said Jess and a man."

"I'm taking you to Carbon City."

"What for?"

"Put you in jail. For what you did."

I stepped out then and told him to shut up with

his bawling and told Wash to cut it short with his talk.
Because you pass three cabins on the way down, and
four more up the mountainside that you can't see but
they see you, and if we ever gave them a chance to
wake up to what was going on we might see something
cutting the leaves. We hustled him down to the car and
Wash drove and I sat on the outside. So when we got to
my cabin, the table was set out under the trees with
some candles on it and both Kady and Jane were looking down the creek to see what had become of us. Wash
began talking to Kady. "Don't wait for us. We'll be
back soon as we can after we get this thing booked,
but don't let the stuff get cold waiting for us."

"Booked? What are you talking about?"

"Didn't he kidnap our boy?"

"He didn't mean any harm."

"It could have cost Danny his life."

"Wash, Moke is a friend of my mother's, and she's
not well, and maybe she needs him. He's not any more
than half-witted anyhow, no matter what he did, so why
can't we forget it and go about our business instead of
putting him in jail for the next five or ten years, where's
he's not any good to anybody?"

"Maybe I'm not so half-witted as you think."

"Maybe a skunk don't stink."

It was me that said that, and then I told her there
were some things that can't be forgotten, and that Moke
was lucky we didn't shoot him, as that's what he had
coming to him. But while I was talking she kept looking at me, and then she said: "Jess, you've had plenty
to say since I've been living here about things that had
to be fought if they were wrong and they were in you,
and all I've got to say is that remembering things long
after they do you any harm is another thing that peo-

ple might fight a little bit, specially if they live up the
creeks in this part of the country, and got the habit of
remembering things long after anybody could remember
what they were trying to remember."

"Do we take him in, Jess?"

"Let's go."

He had cut his motor, but now he started it again,
and she stood aside. "All right, Wash, but you're taking
a lot of trouble for nothing."

"You think it's for nothing?"

"He's not yet your child."

"He will be tomorrow."

"I'm not talking about what he will be. I'm talking
about what he is, and what he was when he was taken.
If they ask me, I'll tell them I've got nothing to say,
and if the mother won't sign the writ, that ends it, unless
of course the child has a father."

"Kady, why are you standing up for Moke?"

"Jess, are you crazy? Who's standing up for Moke?
I'm standing up for myself, and for my little boy that
nobody else is thinking about that I can see. Do you
think I want this in the papers, and then have it come
out that Danny is what they call a love child, and God
knows what else they would think up to put in?"

"It's not any piece for the papers."

"A *kidnapping?*"

She stepped up to the window and talked straight at
Wash. "Haven't you done enough to me without this,
and for no reason except to give a simple-looking imi-
tation of a West Virginia bad man?"

"I'm turning him over to the law."

"You can't even do that, right."

"So you know a better way?"

"You're turning him over to Carbon County when

the crime was committed in Blount? Gee, but you're
smart, aren't you? Gee, but you're going to look wonderful when you get to Carbon City with him and they
say, sorry, son, you're in the right church but the wrong
pew. Gee——"

"Suppose you shut up."

For a minute, steel had been facing steel, but now
they weren't anything but a pair of kids jawing at each
other, and next thing they were laughing and he got
out and she said he was so dumb it was pitiful but there
was no steam in it and the fight was over. So I got out
and told Moke to get out of there and get quick. So he
got out and started up the creek. So Wash, he ran after
him and gave him a kick that knocked him over on his
face. So he got up and began to cuss out Wash, mean,
whispering cusswords, all covered with spit. That was
when Kady walked over and slapped his face, and told
him he'd got off pretty lucky. He stood there panting,
and once or twice he started to say something, and
didn't. But when Jane got his banjo, where it had been
pitched in the car, he went.

But there was one thing that could make us all feel
good, no matter what had been said, and that was
Danny. When Jane brought him out for a little whiff
of air before tucking him in for the night, we were
laughing and talking to him and me and Wash were
taking turns holding him. And then without anybody
knowing he was going to do it, he turned to Wash and
stead of the goo-goo stuff he'd been saying, he said
"Wash," and laughed. It was the first word he ever said,
and it made us all so happy we didn't look at each other
at all, and Kady picked him up and held him close, and
pretty soon he said it again, like he was pretty proud

of himself. And then we heard a car, and down the road
I see the white tow car from the filling station on the
state road that the fellow uses now and then to haul
passengers up the creek for fifty cents. And it stopped
and somebody got out and it went away and we all
stood there trying to see who was coming up the path,
a little satchel in her hand. And then I could feel my
heart sink, because that funny walk, go three steps fast
and then shuffle one, couldn't be but one person. That
was Belle.

"Jess, what *is* she doing here?"
"It's got me buffaloed."
When supper was over, Kady and Wash went for a
ride, and when Belle went to bed, Jane and I took a
walk down the creek. Once Belle got there the party
was ruined, because the half dirty Morgan jokes started
right away, and the way she dressed made you feel the
place had turned into a joint. I don't know what she
did to clothes, but soon as she got them on they weren't
clean any more, and they let you see more than you
wanted to see. All she would take for supper was milk,
and she kept explaining she had had to see Danny before Wash and Kady went away, though when they
were going away, if they were going away, was something that nobody but her seemed to know about. And
how much attention she paid to Danny, now at last she
could see him once more, was about one look and a
wave of the hand. In between, she seemed to be thinking about something, and even the dirty jokes didn't get
the pounding she generally gave them. Belle always told
a joke three times, once to tell it, once to tell it over
again because maybe you didn't understand it, and

once to holler and whoop at how funny it was. So when Jane fixed her a place to sleep in the front room, and she said she wanted to turn in, nobody put up any argument. Wash was staying at the Black Diamond Hotel in Carbon City, but he and Kady wanted to talk how they would get married, so they went off in his car, and Jane and I took our walk, trying to figure out Belle. "She's quite a lot thinner, Jane, and don't look like a fat little wood pigeon any more, but at that she don't look so bad, considering it's eighteen years since she went away."

"At night she don't."

"Of course candle light is not like sun."

"It's not the light, it's the fever. In the evening, when she's running over two degrees, her eyes are bright and her cheeks are red and she really looks pretty. But in the morning, when she's running below normal, she looks awful. Her face is gray, she coughs all the time, and her eyes have that look they get, like they see something far off."

"All this is the consumption?"

"She's got it, bad."

"I'm sorry."

"But what's she doing here?"

"If you ask me, it's got nothing to do with us, and nothing to do with Danny. Any time you try to figure Belle out, you can begin with Moke and go on from there."

"I don't think so."

"She's changed, then."

"She and Moke haven't got along since Danny came. Until then she didn't pay any attention to what Kady and I thought about him, and they got along all right.

But soon as Danny came they started to fight, and there's more to it than they ever let on to anybody but themselves."

"Like what?"

"I don't know."

7

How LONG it had gone on I don't know, but it seemed that all my life I had heard it, this voice out there in the night, calling my name and beating on the door of the cabin. I wasn't in the cabin. I was in the stable, asleep in the bunk I used there, so by the time I got outside, Kady was already coming around from the back door. She lit the carbide lamp we had used in the mine, and when the light cut the darkness, there was Moke, whimpering and wailing and slobbering at the mouth. "Kady, I swear to God I never knew she was nowhere near here. I never even knew it was her till I threw her off me, where she was trying to kill me, and lit a match and seen the blood."

"What blood?"

"From her mouth! It's pouring out."

"You know what to do with her when she gets taken like that. Did you do it, or are you scared so bad you forgot everything?"

"I left her lay, right on the floor of my shack, just like I'm supposed to do, and come on down here for help. I run all the way. But she's never had nothing like this before."

"It's her lung, Jess."

"I know. I'll get a doctor."

"No, the first thing is to run me up there to his shack or as close as we can get to it. Then you run into Carbon City for a doctor, and the best way is to wake up Wash and have him bring the hotel doctor. But leave that part to him. You get back here right away with the main thing, which is ice, to pack her side in, so it chills the blood, and makes a clot inside, to stop that bleeding. Lots of it. Cracked ice if you can get it, but any kind of ice right away is better than waiting around for them to crack it up for you."

We got moving fast, then. She went inside, put on a coat, and went through Belle's bag for all the medicine that was in it. I went back to where Jane had been listening at the window, and told her she was to stay there with Danny no matter how long we were gone. Then I had her help me move Kady's bed on the truck, with sheets and all like it was, because in that shack was nothing but a dirt floor, and even if we weren't allowed to move her she had to have something to lay on. By then Kady was ready and got in and Moke got in. But all that time I had been thinking about what he had said, and the more I thought about it the more it didn't make any sense. "What's that you said about her trying to kill you?"

"You deef and can't hear me?"

"I asked you something."

"She crept in there while I was asleep. I don't know

where she came from. First thing I knew somebody was slashing at me with a knife."

"I don't see any cuts on you."

"You will on the dog."

"What dog?"

"Birdie Blue's puppydog, that was out when I got home, and that I brung in for company. He was laying close to me, where I was sleeping on the gunny sacks, and he took the first stab and maybe some more. She stabbed like a wild woman, and when she felt the knife go in she thought she had me till I wrestled her off and the blood begun coming out of her mouth."

"Why did she do this?"

"I don't know."

"Come on, don't lie to me."

"Suppose you ask her."

There was no asking her anything, though, by the time we got there. By putting one side of the truck on the path and letting the other side bump, I got pretty close to the shack, and she was still laying on the floor, but two or three people from the hollow were there by that time with lanterns, and they were trying to get her up and move her. So the way Kady explained it to me, that was the worst thing in the world, so we stopped it and had those people carry the bed up, and the door was too small for it, but they began putting it up outside, and used the loose log, the one Wash and I had pushed out of the way, to wedge it up level. Then Kady rolled up a sheet to the middle, and laid it down beside Belle, and shoved the rolled part under her, then unrolled it, and we all helped lift and at last she was off the floor and on a bed. But the blood that was in a puddle on the other side of her, and the dead dog that was

laying in the middle of it, you could see all that, and
the blood began to run in a stream toward the door,
and stunk, and it was a mess. So I told one of those
people to take the dog out and bury it, and get started
washing out the blood, but Kady said quit worrying
about that, and get started after the ice. So I burned
the road to the hotel, and called Wash, and told him
to get a doctor out there, and told the man on the desk
I wanted some ice, and be quick about it, so he hopped
pretty lively. Because the last thing I did when I left the
cabin on the way to the hollow was to strap on my .45
that hung across from my rifle, and there's nothing like
having a six-shooter on you to get action when you
want it.

The rest of the night was like a whirl-around dream
you have when you're sick, with the doctor giving her
some kind of stuff to inhale, and Kady tearing up sheets
to make bags for the ice, and more and more people
from the hollow standing around, watching what was
going on and giving help whenever it was wanted. What
they had heard when Belle and Moke were having it
there in the dark, before he came to my place, if they
heard anything at all, I don't know, but by the time
Wash got there with the doctor the dog was gone and
the knife was gone and nothing was said about anybody
trying some killing. All the doctor saw was a woman
bleeding from lung trouble, and so far as what was said
to him went, that's all there was. Around daylight he
got the bleeding stopped, and went home, but before he
went he called Kady off to one side, and Wash and I
drifted over to hear what he said to her.

"You're Mrs. Tyler's daughter, miss?"

"Yes, I am."

"You know what this means?"

"You think she's pretty sick?"

"If I had her in the hospital, where I could force-feed her with what she needs, sock a couple of quarts of blood into her, and then when she's in shape, collapse that lung for her, I might pull her through for a few more months, or even years. But I can't do it here, and by the time I got her to town she'd be dead. She's on the end of the plank. It could come any time now, but she'll probably last until tonight. Her mouth temperature is down to 97, and I can't get it up on account of the ice that has to stay there. It'll slip to 96, and then it'll take a sudden drop. With that she'll go in the coma, and then it's just a matter of when."

"We've more or less expected it."

"Call me, and I'll sign the papers."

"I'll do it from the filling station on the state road."

She was looking up at the trees, and was waxy color from losing the blood, but Kady had combed her hair out nice and put a ribbon in it, and just for a minute, with the sun coming up and the birds starting to sing, she looked like she had when I first saw her, in church one night, just after her father moved to town to work in the mine. She was looking up then too, and singing *Stand Up, Stand Up for Jesus,* and I kept looking at her, and next thing I knew she was looking at me, and winking. We got married the next month, she fourteen, I four years older, just the regular age for a coal camp. It seemed funny, after all that had happened, she was still only thirty-nine years old. After a while she put out her hand and took mine, where I was sitting near by. "Jess, I'm going to die."

"We're doing all we can."

"I know, but I'm going to die."

"I'm awful sorry, Belle."

"I'm not. I made a mess of my life, Jess."

"You lived it like you wanted it."

"I lived it like I liked it, but not like I wanted it. We could have been happy, you and me, because we loved each other, and that's enough. But I was born to mess things up, and I began to hold things against you. That you went to church, and believed what you heard there, and took things serious, and never took a drink. I thought that was all a pack of foolishness, and after I got the taste for liquor I couldn't hardly stand you at all. And I began doing things. I did a lot more than I ever told you, Jess. And then I started up with Moke. Ten of him wasn't worth what you was, and I knew it, but I couldn't help how I was going. He sung comical songs at me, and we'd meet by the creek and drink applejack, and when I'd come home I'd be so I could hardly stand up, and have to pretend I was sick after I chewed sassafras root so you wouldn't smell my breath. And then I went off with him."

"If he made you happy, I'm glad."

"He didn't."

"More than you think, maybe."

"Maybe worse than I could have imagined."

She closed her eyes, and I thought there would be more, and at last I would know what she had come up here for, and why she had tried to kill Moke, and why he had stolen Danny, and all the rest of what had been going on the last few days that I didn't understand. But she just asked if she could see Danny and I ran down in the truck to the cabin, and as soon as Jane could get him ready we brought him up. She looked at him a long time, and talked to him, and took his hand and played

with it. All that time I was holding him. I liked that
better than anything I had ever had in my life, and she
must have seen it because she said: "You love him,
don't you, Jess?"

"Love's no word for it."

"I want you to."

She began to cough then, and sank back on the pil-
low, and Kady came up in case there was trouble. But
what I noticed was Moke, sitting there in the door of
the shack, looking at me with such hate in his eyes I
don't think I ever saw in a man before.

She called for the girls and said good-by to them, and
when she talked to Kady she ran her fingers over her
face, and looked up at her with an expression that hit
me in the throat somewhere, because it was beautiful,
and I was glad, because maybe you could understand
why things had come between, but they were her
daughters, and now she was going, both sides should
feel some love.

And then she called for Moke, and he never even
raised his head. "Moke, I want to talk to you."

"I got nothing to say to you."

"Moke, I'm dying."

"Then die."

"Moke, I've loved you, and there's something I've
got to ask of you, and it's my right to do it, and you've
got to listen to me."

"I won't."

"Then, Moke, will you sing to me once?"

To that he didn't say anything for a minute, then he
came over to her and put his head on her shoulder and
let her pat him and whisper in his ear. And if he sang
to her I don't know. The last I saw of them, they were

together up there, and I ran down to the cabin and watched Danny with Jane while he had his nap. Then Birdie Blue rode up on a mule, and told us Kady sent word to phone the doctor.

8

IT WAS LATE AFTERNOON when I got to Tulip with the doctor, and Kady was there at the church, and she and I waited while he went up to certify the death or whatever it is they do. In a minute a wagon came up the creek with two men in it, and they had a tool chest from the old drift mouth of the mine. They went on up to a cabin, and pretty soon here came the sound of hammering. "You hear that, Jess?"

"What are they up to?"

"They're making a casket."

"Who asked them to?"

"Moke I guess."

"What's he got to do with it?"

"He's burying her."

"Him and who else?"

"These women here, these relations of his, they've already got her washed, and soon as the doctor gets through they're going to lay her out."

"Funny they didn't speak to me about it."

"Is there any reason they should?"

"Before the law, she was my wife."

"Before God, she was his."

"He certainly didn't act much like it."

"They made up their quarrel, whatever it was about. He loved her, even if he is such a poor excuse for a man, and it seems to me you don't have to get up on your ear and be onry just because you don't like him."

"I loved her once."

"This is now."

Three boys came down the hill with bunches of laurel, for the funeral, and Kady took them inside the church and showed them where to put it. I knew them all, Lew Cass, Bobby Hunter, and Luke Blue, but I didn't pay any attention to it till later that not one of them spoke to me.

In the morning Mr. Rivers, that was doing the preaching, stopped by in his car to take us up to the church. Kady got in, and Jane got in with Danny, and I started to get in. "Hold on, Jess. Nothing was said about you."

"Does there have to be?"

"Well now I don't know."

"I don't need any special invitation."

I got in, and he sat there holding the wheel a minute or two, like he was thinking, then he drove on. In the clearing by the church were some cars and that's where he parked. The girls got out with the baby and we all started for the church. "Hold on, not so fast."

Ed Blue came out with three or four others, and they had rifles. "It's all right for Kady and Jane and the baby. But Jess, he stays out."

"Who says so?"

"Moke."

Kady and Jane looked at each other, and after a while Kady said: "Jess, I think it's awful of him, and if I could I'd leave with you, right now. But it's my mother. I can't just turn my back on her."

"That how you feel, Jane?"

"Yes, Jess."

"Then there's nothing I can do but go, but you're not taking Danny in there. That runt stole him once, and maybe he takes some other fool notion now. I'm taking him home."

"Maybe you better."

When I got back to the house with him, walking, Wash was there, in his car, reading the morning paper.

"Funeral too much for him hey?"

"It wasn't him, it was me."

When he heard what had happened, he cussed and raved and said we should each take a gun and go up there and clean the place out.

"We can't do it, Wash."

"Why not?"

"In the first place, it's a funeral, and it's entitled not to be busted up by any shooting. And in the second place, if I start anything like that, I got to leave Danny, and they'll find some way to get back at me by getting back on him."

"I'd forgot about that."

He marched up and down by the creek, snapping his fingers, and then pretty soon he went in the cabin and came out with my rifle.

"Don't worry, I won't do any more than I have to. But we still got that little lookout back of his cabin, that I can get to up through the woods without being seen, and when he gets back from the church we're going to start right where we left off. I'm going to throw down on him, and he's coming with me, and he's going right off to jail, where he was headed before. What he's forgot is that he's still the kidnapper of my boy, and if Blount's where I've got to take him, I got all day, and not any stuff about Danny not having a name is going to stop me this time. He'll have a name in plenty time for the grand jury to do their stuff."

And he went up the path through the woods. But when he came back he was alone.

"Jess, you remember why we picked that spot?"

"So we could hear."

"And I heard everything. I could hear every word the preacher said, and the hymns they sung, and somebody crying. And then, when I crept out to the bank of the gully and looked down, I could see them all. They came out of the church, six men, carrying a little gray casket."

"Made from a tool chest they stole."

"That's just about it. They had taken two pieces of rope, and stapled them along each side, so they had handholds. They carried it to the graveyard back of the church, and there they had some more preaching. Then they lowered it with two other pieces of rope into the grave. Then it broke up. And then I got my gun ready, because here came Moke, up the gully to his shack, alone. But Kady called him, and came running up to say good-by. He didn't pay much attention to her, and said he had heard she was going to get married, and he'd see her at the wedding. And she said she had decided to get married in town, in Carbon City, the first I had heard of it."

"First I heard of it too."

"She had wanted it in that little church."

"Until they kicked me out."

"That's probably it. So he said all right, he'd come to the cabin, and ride in to the church with her. She said there might not be room. He said he'd go in on the bus. And then, Jess, do you know what she said?"

"I'm listening."

"She said, 'Moke, at my wedding I only want friends, though I've tried to treat you as decent as I know how on account of my mother. And if you show up, I'm going to ask Jess to do to you exactly what you did to him. Keep you out, if he's got to take a rifle to do it. Good-by and good luck, but from now on, you keep out of my life.' "

"What did he say to that?"

"What could he say?"

"He took it?"

"He turned around and went in his shack. And Jess, maybe you think I'm a yellow quitting dog, but that satisfies me if it does you."

"It satisfies me."

"Then to hell with him."

"Like she said, let's kick him out of our life."

We shook hands, and he ran in to hang up the rifle again, before the girls got back and Kady found out what he'd been up to.

"Jess, are you happy?"

"For the first time in my life."

"Me too, I just can't believe it. Is it wrong to feel like that, the very same night you buried your mother?"

"Why would it be?"

"Maybe this is how it should be, Jess. That one part of my life should begin just when the other part ends.

Because if there's one part of me I've got to fight, like you always told me, it's no trouble to figure out where it came from. And that part we just buried. And tomorrow, I start a new life. With the other part of me. And it's no trouble to figure out where that came from, either. You gave in a little bit, Jess. But no more than you had to, to keep me home, and out of the devilment I was sliding into. On the big things, you fought it out, and made me fight it out. If I'm beholden to anybody for anything, it's to you for that, Jess. I'll always be."

She put her hand in mine, with the moon hanging over the woods and making the creek look like silver. "I love you, Kady."

"And I love you, Jess. And I'm so proud of you."

"I hate it that you're going, but I'm glad."

"I've cost you money, Jess."

"No, you haven't."

"That still and all."

"That still, so far as I'm concerned, it's not even up there. We took in some money, a lot more than we spent. I blew out a lot of stumps, to put more corn in, and they were on my own land, and now I've got the new clearing, and I can grow more on it. I can put in more stock any time I want, and I got the cash to buy it. So stop talking about costing me money, or saying any more about it. We broke the law, but nobody's the worse off, and it all worked in together to bring us both a whole lot more happiness than we were ever going to have if we'd never met up and did like we did."

"You like Wash?"

"He's a fine boy."

"You coming to see us?"

"Any time I'm asked."

"You will be, because he loves you."

"I want Jane with us."

"Me too."

We went to the window and called, and Jane slipped on a dress and came out, and that was the first it came to us there was no more home in Blount, now that Belle had died and Moke had left it. And then we decided that Jane should move in and live with me, and that made it wonderful. "And specially with me here, because you can have Kady lend us Danny now and then, when she's going up to Philadelphia to visit her rich friends, and I can take care of him and you can teach him how to ride."

She was laughing at me, but I wouldn't have it that way. "It's not on account of Danny at all. It's on account of you, Jane. On account of both of us. We'll be happy."

"But we'll have Danny, sometimes."

"Then all right."

Kady got to laughing by then, and we all started laughing, and then we all got some Coca-Cola and drank it, and held hands.

"And I'm glad of one thing."

"What's that, Kady?"

"That I'm not going to be married in that church up there, where we held the funeral today. That's what I'm trying to get away from. The one I picked out, the Methodist Church in Carbon, is pretty. It's gray stone, with a square tower in front, and it's what I'm going to."

"That's right."

"And I've ordered flowers."

"What kind?"

Jane was so excited we were going to have regular

flowers from a florist she had a flutter in her eyes. And when Kady told us how they were going to put lilies and things all around inside, I was glad too, and it seemed to me that was really the right place for her to go, and it was all going to turn out wonderful.

9

I WAS UP before dawn, and got all my feeding and milking and cleaning done, and put on my best suit, and we had our breakfast. Then I took a rest while they worked, because they had to get Danny ready and get dressed themselves. Then women began dropping by from all up and down the creek, and they had to have it explained to them all over again, how Wash would come out around noon and take the girls and Danny in, while I would follow along in the truck, so I could take Jane back, while Kady and Wash would go over to the hotel with Danny and change into other clothes, so they could drive off some place. So then there was a lot of talk about the flowers Wash was going to bring, and I had never worn one in my life, but I thought for Kady's wedding I would put one in my buttonhole. So I knew where some wild roses were, down the creek a way, at the edge of a piece of woods, and started down there. But I didn't more than get started when up on the mountainside I saw something move. Now so far as I was concerned, that still up there I knew nothing about, had never seen, and never heard of. But that was so far as I was concerned. So far as an officer was concerned maybe I was the fellow that lived closest to it. Or maybe I had left something up there and forgotten about it. Or maybe when I talked to him I'd have got a funny look on my face. I had to know who it was, because there was no regular business anybody could have up there, fifteen feet from the shaft mouth, but nowhere near anything else.

I crossed the creek on some stones, kept under the cliff so I couldn't be seen, and hit the path that led up to the timbered drift, the one we had used to roll our stuff into after we hauled it up on a block and falls from the road. About a hundred feet inside was a tool chest where I kept extra lamps, water, carbide, canned beans, and some dynamite, in case I had to shoot the tunnel down and get out quick through the shaft. It was the first I had been there since Jane came with Danny, and already I hated it that I had ever had anything to do with the liquor. Because the mash I had left fermenting was so high it turned your stomach to smell it, and the rats that had come in for our grain almost knocked me down jumping off the bins to get out of my way. You don't kill rats in a mine, because if something's going to happen they know it before God knows it, and the way they run out with men right on their tail, they're called the miner's best friend. Just the same, they turned my stomach worse than the smell.

I watched for a minute, but I didn't see anything so I started up the ladder, first putting out the light. Then I came down and took off my shoes. Then I went up again, and when I got to the top I raised my head easy, because if a deputy marshal would have me covered, or what would be there, I didn't exactly know. But it was no officer. It was Moke, and across his knees was the same Winchester Ed Blue had thrown on me the day before, when he wouldn't let me in the church. And where he was sitting was the one spot on the mountainside where he could cover a sharp bend in the road, where I'd have to come almost to a stop, on my way in to the wedding. I held my breath, because if he ever saw me I'd never make it down the ladder before he stepped over and plugged me. And then my heart stopped beating, and I almost fell down the shaft. Because it was hot, and he had taken off the jumper of his denims, so he was bare from the waist up. And I could see why Belle had fought with him over Danny, why he had kidnapped the boy, why he hated Wash, and all the rest of it, or thought I could.

By his navel was the butterfly.

When I got back to the cabin both girls were up the road with Danny, saying good-by to a woman that lived up the creek. Jane had on a dress, but Kady had on nothing but shoes and stockings and pants, with nothing over them but a blue checked apron she had slipped on to go out in. I waited while the woman, that was named Liza Minden, told it how she had known all the Blounts before Wash's father had owned a mine or anything, and how they were wonderful people, and Kady was going to like them fine. And the more she went on, the crazier I got. I took down my rifle and loaded it, and waited some more. Then I went to the window— and leveled it, and drew a bead on her. I meant to shoot her through the heart for what she was, a rotten little slut that would even go to bed with her own father if he

would let her, and that had already gone to bed with
her mother's lover, and was getting ready to marry a
boy that was no more relation to the child she said was
his than a possum was. But when I sighted the gun I
couldn't pull the trigger. I went outside, so I wouldn't
see her any more, and my feet lifted high off the ground
when I walked, like I had just been hung and was
dancing on air.

"Jess, you're crazy."
"No, I'm not."
"Everybody's got birthmarks."
"Wash, if the birthmark was all, I might not pay any
attention to it either. But it's not. Ever since Jane got
here and found the boy in his shack, I've been trying
to figure out why he kidnapped him, and so have you
and so has everybody. Ever since Belle came in that
night, I've been trying to figure out what she was doing
there, and since she tried to kill Moke, I've been trying
to figure out why. So have you, so has Jane, so has
everybody. All right, now we know. He kidnapped
Danny because Danny's his child, and he knew it from
the birthmark and so did Belle, and so did Kady. But
Jane got him back, and then Kady had the chance to
marry you, if she could ever keep it dark about this
other thing. But Belle knew Moke better than anybody
else knew him. She knew if it was the last chance he
had, Moke would spill it. And she didn't have much
longer to live anyhow, so she came up here to stop him,
the only way she knew. And what the hell do you
mean, everybody has birthmarks? How could a baby
and a man have a birthmark like that and it not mean
anything?"
He was sitting on the edge of the bed in his hotel

room, all dressed for the wedding except for his coat, that was on the back of a chair with a carnation in the buttonhole, and two boxes of flowers in the same chair. He lit a cigarette and smoked a long time. Then he said: "Listen, Jess, it just can't be true. In the first place she's not that kind of a girl. And if she was that kind of a girl, she couldn't be that kind of a girl with Moke. And he's old enough to be her father. He's almost as old as you are, Jess."

"He's thirty-nine."

"Then she couldn't fool around with him."

"Yes, she could."

"Jess, I say she couldn't."

He snapped that at me with a killer light in his eye, and I don't know what kind of a look I had in my eye when I slung it back at him, but it must have said something, because he staggered back against the wall and said, "Jesus Christ."

"You think I'm just fooling?"

He lit another cigarette and thought a while, and said: "Then I've got to kill him, Jess."

"That I won't let you do."

"I wasn't asking you."

"You don't know where he is and I won't tell you and even if you did know you couldn't get to him without a guide. And by the time you find one, if you can find one, he'll be dead, because I'm going to kill him on my way back."

"She's the mother of my—"

He broke off and looked at me, and I think it was the first time he got it through his head, the meaning of what I had told him.

"I really got nothing to do with it, have I?"

"Not a thing in this world."

"Unless—"

"You killed *her,* is that it?"

He didn't answer me. He just went and looked out the window, but that was what he had started to say. "Well, Wash, I tried it, but I couldn't."

"I could."

"Him, that'll be different."

There came a ring on his buzzer and he opened the door. It was his father and mother. His father was tall, like he was, with gray hair and a brown, sunburned face. But his mother was pink and pretty and sweet, and went over to him and kissed him and asked if the bride was here, and where was the baby, and lots more stuff like that. He said who I was, and both of them shook hands, and said they had hoped I'd be able to get to the wedding.

"There won't be any wedding, Mom."

"What?"

"Sorry you took the trip all for nothing. Now we're going home."

10

WHEN I GOT NEAR the bend I stopped, hid the truck
back of the old filling station, got the rifle out, and
crossed the creek on the pillars of the old bridge. I kept
on up on the other side, keeping under the cliff and
out of sight from above till I came to the path. Then
I crept up the mountainside without making any noise
at all. When I came to the drift I went in, opened the
tool chest, refilled the lamp, lit it, and set it down. I
cut off about six feet of fuse, rolled it up, and stuck
it in my pocket. I put a box of caps in there with it. I
stuck a couple of sticks of dynamite in my pocket on
the other side. Then I went on in. When I came to the
shaft I laid out powder, fuse, and caps on a scaffold,
and put my shoes beside them, tied to a scantling against
rats. Then I picked up the rifle and started up the
ladder. When I lifted my head out he had moved, with
the sun, about six feet away from where he had been
before, but that put him facing me more, and made it

better. He was eating beans out of a can with his knife, and I let him finish them up before I raised my gun. I drew my bead right on the butterfly. He doubled up when I pulled the trigger, and held on to his stomach, and kicked like a cat trying to shake papers off its feet, and drew his breath in and out fast like a dog in the summer time, except instead of heat that made him do that, it was pain. That suited me fine. I stepped out, picked up his rifle from where he had set it down to eat, and sat down to watch him twitch.

"You dirty son of a bitch."

"Hello, Moke."

"God, that would be like you, Jess, to shoot me in the belly and then go on and leave me here to die."

"Oh, I wouldn't go off and leave you, if that's all that's worrying you. There's buzzards up there, and I couldn't have them flying around to tip anybody off."

"Couldn't you shoot me through the heart?"

"I shoot you where you got it coming."

"What the hell are you talking about?"

"I let you off once, because I thought neither you nor the woman was worth it. But now you went too far, and I got to teach you to lay off my daughter."

"Your *what?*"

"You heard me."

"Say, that's a joke."

"I shot you in the butterfly. That's what little Danny's got, isn't it? Isn't that what you did for your country? Leave a poor little kid that's birthmarked like you? Well, you don't do it with my daughter and live to tell about it."

"Kady never done nothing with me."

"I'll attend to her, later."

"You going to attend to Danny?"

"I'll take care of him, anyway."

"You like Danny, don't you?"

"That's none of your damned business."

"The hell it's not. Yeah, you'll attend to Kady. You'll hit her with a harness trace, and put her out, and act just like you always acted, with that religion-crazy disposition you got. But you won't put Danny out, oh no. You'll keep him, and let Jane take care of him, because you're crazy about him. No matter what she done, he's yours. Kady's nothing but a woman, and you never knew how to treat one. But Danny, oh yes, I seen you with him up there yesterday, when Belle was dying. You never seen nothing as pretty as he is, did you? He's yours, no matter what Kady done. He's your grandchild, ain't he? Well now you get it, you rotten, belly-shooting, dumb son of a bitch. He's not yours. He's mine."

"What did you say?"

"That butterfly, yeah, we got a butterfly in my family. But only the men got it, see? If the child's a girl, it skips. It skips to the next boy. He's not your grandchild, Jess, *he's mine!*"

He raised up on one elbow to shove his face closer to mine, then fell back from the pain and held both hands over his stomach and drew his legs up tight over his hands. "Jesus Christ, stuff is coming out of me!"

"What's that you said?"

"Get a doctor, stuff is coming out with the blood!"

"Never mind the stuff! Talk!"

I got up and hauled off my foot to kick him where he was holding his hands, but he began to scream and said he'd talk but to get him some water or he can't stand it any more. I climbed down the ladder, dipped up some cold spring water in the bucket, put on my shoes and came on back up. Sweat was on his face when I filled the cup and give it to him to drink. He took it in one hand, then began to puke.

"The stuff that's all over my hand, it stinks!"

"Here."

I held the cup and let him wash out his mouth and drink three or four cupfuls. Then I poured water over his belly to wash off the stuff and the blood and the bugs that had got in it. "Now spit it out, what I asked you, and spit quick."

"I told you all I'm telling you."

"That Danny's your grandson?"

"You're goddam right. We never knew it, Belle and I, for twenty years, that Kady was ours, until Danny came, and we seen the butterfly. Then we knew."

"So Belle two-timed me even before she left."

"The way you treated her why not?"

"I loved her. What more did she want?"

"Yeah, you loved her. If she'd go to church three times on Sunday and pray every night and look at your sour face all the rest of the time, you loved her. Well who she loved was me. Because she liked a good time. And me, I had a banjo."

"That was something, wasn't it?"

"To Belle it was. You bet she two-timed you."

He called for more water, and I gave him some, and he cussed me out, and began calling Kady every dirty name he could think of. "She hated Danny. She hated him because his father walked out on her, and she's been so proud and stuck-up she couldn't stand it she was just a girl like anybody else. But I loved him." And then, after a while: "Belle was going crazy from fear I would spill it to Kady whose child she really was, and

if I did, she would hate Belle. So that was late afternoon, and Belle caught the bus, to come up here and
kill me. If it had been morning she wouldn't have done
it. The fever, it came on as the day wore on. It made her
crazy. After she come in my shack that night, and I
knew she was going to die, I thought I'd wait till that
was over, and then come out with it. It was all I had to
live for. Why should I keep my mouth shut? Why
should I give a hoot how Kady felt? She never cared
how *I* felt. But Belle knew what she could do with me.
She got me to come over there, just before she died,
after you left and Kady left and they took Danny away,
and promise I'd never say anything to Kady about it.
So that's what I done. I give up the one thing I wanted
in life, to please a woman that was dying, and that I
loved. But I made up my mind, if I had to give it up,
you'd give it up too. You weren't going to be happy
with something that was mine. So I got Ed Blue's gun,
and I'd have killed you, Jess. That's the only thing I'm
sorry for, that you got me first. But by Jesus Christ, I'm
going to take it away from you, that one thing that you
want. I never promised not to tell you, and now I'm
letting you have it. There's not one drop of Tyler blood
in Danny, and you've just been making a fool out of
yourself to think there is. Come here, you samsinging
bastard, and let me spit on you."

I put his jumper over his chest, crossed the arms
over his back, and tied them up tight. Then I used
them for a handle and began dragging him.

"Stop it! That hurts!"

"It won't, much longer."

"Where you taking me?"

"You'll see."

I drug him to the shaft, and when he saw what I was

going to do he began to scream. I slung him in, and he
screamed clear to the bottom, but stopped when he hit.
I slung Mort's rifle in after him, and stepped back in
case it would go off. When it didn't I picked up my own
gun and climbed down. He was at the bottom, all
crumpled up, beside the bricked-in fireplace of the still.
I tied the jumper on him better, lit the lamp, and began
dragging him along the tunnel. But when I came to the
first of the old entries I turned off, and began dragging
him over the jagged rock that had fallen down, and it
was the hardest work I ever did in my life. But it felt
good, too, to know he was dead, and I had killed him,
and I was going to put him where he never would be
found, and nobody would ever remember he had been
on this earth. I drug him at least two hundred feet.
Then there was a swag, and I threw him in. Then I
climbed back to the timbered tunnel, went on back to
the shaft, took a bucket, scraped up some dirt and put
it in, poured in some water, and mixed up some mud.
Then I took my fuse, càps, and dynamite, stuck them
in my pocket, and went back to the swag with them.
The first blister that was hanging down on the other
side, between the swag and the worked-out part of the
mine, I cut off half a stick of dynamite, made a mudcap against one of the hanging pieces, stuck the dynamite in with a cap in it and six inches of fuse. The blister
between the swag and the timbered drift, I made another
mudcap, with a foot of fuse. Then I went in, lit the
short fuse, scrambled to the next one and lit it, and
stepped around to the angle of the timbered tunnel to
wait. Why I had done that, I wanted those shots not
to fire at once, and then I could check that they both
went off. Sure enough, here came the first one. Then I
almost dropped dead, because I had forgot the rifle.

I ran to the shaft mouth, got it, and coming back I ran sidewise like a crab, the way you have to do in a low tunnel. Smoke was pouring out of the tunnel, but I crawled in there and gave the rifle a pitch. Before I got to the timbered drift the second shot went off, and blew me right up against the rib. Then I was glad I had had to make the second trip in, for the rifle. Because by going in there I had seen what I'd always have been worried about. That powder had blown down the top until the tunnel was blocked up solid with rock, both sides of Moke, so it would take a hundred men a month to get in there, even if they could ever guess what they were digging for. Mr. Moke Blue could just as well have been at the bottom of the sea, so far as anybody in this world could ever find him.

When I got to the creek I took the empty shell out of my gun, threw it in the water, and put a fresh one in the chamber. Then I cut a switch and peeled it, and rammed a piece of my handkerchief through the bore, to clean it, so it hadn't been fired since it was loaded. Then I went down and pitched it on the truck and started over to Blount, to tell Wash what Moke had told me. I was already halfway over there, before it came to me what it meant, if what he said was true.

She wasn't my daughter any more!

11

I CUT MY LIGHTS, ran in behind the old filling station again, and hid the truck like I had before. I crept on up the road without making any noise, and the first thing I did was look in the barn and the stable, and all the stock was inside, but they weren't bellowing or anything, and that meant they'd all been fed and the cows milked. I crept on up to the house and peeped in the front room. I peeped in the back room and Jane was there, with Danny in her lap, but no sign of Kady. Pretty soon Danny began to cry, and when Jane bent over him and began to rock him I saw she was crying too. "Little baby, that's always been treated so bad! Ever since his first day on earth he's been put on and stolen and left all alone and kicked around. Don't cry, little boy. Don't you mind a bit, my little Danny. I'm here. I'll always be here, and I'll always love you no matter what your mother does or your father does or anybody does."

It made a lump come in my throat, but I went down to the truck and got in and drove to town. When I got near the White Horse I parked, and went to a window and looked in. She was there, like I knew she would be, dancing with a man I had never seen, and plenty drunk, by her looks. I rubbed my hands on my coat, to wipe off the sweat, and went inside. I didn't pay any attention to her. I went to a booth and sat down. When a waiter came I ordered a drink and when he brought it I took a sip. Pretty soon I could feel her standing beside me. "Well this is quite a surprise."

"Oh. Hello, Kady."

"What are you doing here, Jess?"

"Just having me a corn and Coca-Cola."

"Since when did you take a drink?"

"Sometimes you need it."

"When, for instance?"

"Like when you expect to give a girl away, at her wedding, and she runs out on you and leaves you holding the bag there at the church and don't even come around to tell you why, then you feel like you could drink quite a little."

"You were at the church?"

"If you were eloping, why couldn't you tell me?"

"I didn't elope."

"All right then, get married somewhere else."

"Does it look like I got married?"

I cut out the thick talk then and really looked at her, and made her sit down across the table from me, and ordered her a drink.

"Kady, we got our lines crossed somehow. I been sick all afternoon, that you would just go off and leave me after all we'd been to each other, but if you didn't get married, it don't square up with what I thought. What happened?"

"We'll begin with what happened to you."

"Nothing happened to me."

"You were to follow us in to town in the truck, and instead of that you just disappeared and I can't get it out of my head that you doing that has some connection with what happened to me."

"Didn't you see me wigwag?"

"I didn't see anything."

"I went down to get myself a flower to put in my buttonhole from the woods across the creek, and I slipped on a stone and got mud on my shoe. If it was some other time I'd have given it a brush and a grease, but for your wedding I wanted a shine. But when I got back to the house Liza Minden was there, and I knew if she ever saw me I'd be an hour getting her to go, so I went inside and went to the window, where I was behind her and you could see me, and wigwagged at you I was going to town now, instead of later."

"If you did, I didn't notice it."

"You were looking right at me, and nodded."

"Why did you take that gun?"

"Just in case."

"Case of what?"

"After what they did yesterday at the funeral how did I know what they might try? It didn't cost anything to pitch the gun on the truck, so I did. It's still there."

". . . Did you see Wash?"

"It's like I told you. I went in to get a shine, and where I got it was a barber shop. I had me a haircut too, and by then it was getting on to one o'clock. I supposed he had started by then, so I went on around to the church to wait for you and him and Jane, when you got there. Nobody was there, but I didn't think anything of it, and sat down. I waited quite a while before I began to get worried. Then I went around to his hotel and asked for him."

"When was that?"

"About two o'clock."

"What did they tell you?"

"That he'd left, with a lady and gentleman."

By her face, I knew that stead of not believing what I was saying, she was believing it. I shut up then, and talked when she talked to me, for fear I'd overplay it.

"You thought that was me?"

"I thought I wasn't good enough for you."

"It was his mother and father."

"I still don't know what happened."

"He just didn't come."

"Why not?"

"Do I know?"

"He just walked out on you?"

"I know what happened. Of course I do. They talked it over one last time, his father and that awful mother he's got, and changed their minds once more."

"Hasn't he got a mind of his own?"

"He thinks she's wonderful."

We each drank our drink, and had a couple more, and she sat there with a sour little smile on her face, looking into her glass. "Funny life, isn't it, Jess?"

"Treats you funny all right."

"Who gives a damn?"

"I don't like to hear you cuss."

"Come on, let's dance."

"I never danced."

"I'll teach you."

But I didn't need much teaching, because all we did was stand in the middle of the floor in each other's arms and swing in time to the music and touch our faces together and sometimes walk around a little bit. She had a hot place around her mouth that crept out until her whole cheek felt like she had fever. I inched her along till we were next to the side door and then I lifted her so we were dancing on the parking lot outside and then instead of our cheeks rubbing it was our mouths.

"Jess, let's go to a hotel."

"I'd be afraid."

"What of?"

"We'd have to say we're man and wife."

"Well? You ashamed of me?"

"I hear if they suspicion you at all, like if the man's a lot older than the girl, they ask you for your certificate. And we haven't got one."

"You're a funny guy, Jess."

"What's so funny about me?"

"You're the same old Sunday-go-to-meeting, that thinks we all the time got to be fighting something, and yet you've got to pretend it's something else."

"No, I've changed."

"Your kisses have."

"And I have. Honest."

"And it's only that you're scared?"

"We don't have to be, though."

"How do we fix it that we're not?"

"We could get married."

She gave a whoop and laughed so hard I thought she'd fall down and I'd have to carry her to the truck. "Jess, you ought to get drunk oftener, so it wouldn't do such funny things to you. They won't let us, don't you know that?"

"Why not? We could say, 'no relation.' "

"Not here, we couldn't. Everybody knows me, from the drinks I've served in this honky tonk. And they know you, from that trial we had, with a big bunch looking at you, and specially all the newspaper and courthouse people looking at you."

"All right, then, we'll go to Gilroy."

"Don't they make you tell a whole lot of stuff about who your father and mother were and where you were born and all that? Who would I say?"

". . . Well, how about saying Moke?"

"What?"

For just that long she sobered up, while she looked at me with the kind of fire in her eye a cat gets in front of a light.

"Listen, Jess, I don't say I wouldn't do some crazy things to get you in my arms, because to me you look awful pretty. But don't ever ask me to say that, and don't you even think it. Do you hear me? It was bad enough, having him around my own mother, but having to say I was any part of him would be more than I could stand. I asked you, do you hear me?"

"I hear you."

"What you sulking about?"

"Nothing."

"Do you want me?"

"I'm crazy for you."

"Do you want me bad enough, that if I went down there and held your hand in front of some preacher, you would take me, and not have any more foolish talk about fighting things and hollering hallelujah for fear the devil's going to get you for it?"

"Yes, I do."

"Then couldn't I make up some names?"

Our mouths came together hot this time, and I thought my heart would pump out of my chest from knowing I wouldn't have to give her up any more and at last she was mine.

12

WE STAYED FOR two days in a little Gilroy hotel, and
all that time I kept wondering what we were going to
say when we got home. She must have been doing some
thinking too, because on the way back she said:

"Jess, we're keeping this quiet."

"You mean that we're married?"

"All right, we got drunk and meant it for a joke and
didn't know what we were doing anyway. At least, we
can tell that to a judge if we ever have to, and maybe
he'll believe us. But I don't know any way to tell it to
Jane, and I love her."

"We going to see each other?"

"I'll have to think about that."

"I can't do without you."

"We'll see."

When we got home I acted like I'd been away looking for her all that time, and Jane was so glad to see
her she didn't even think whether it sounded fishy or

not. She kissed me, and was glad to see me all right, but all she thought about was Kady, and how good Kady was going to feel at the nice way she'd kept Danny, and she took Danny in her arms, and talked to him, and listened to him now he practiced up some more words he had learned, or thought he had learned, though what they were was more than I could figure out myself. But that night, after I'd finished up all the work Jane had been doing the two days I'd left everything to her, and had gone to bed in my bunk down in the stable, the door opened and there was Kady, in her nightgown.

"Jess?"

"Come in, Kady."

"I made out I couldn't sleep."

I flipped back the blanket for her to come in with me, but she shook her head and sat on the edge of the bunk looking out the window over my head. After a while she said:

"Jess, what am I going to do about Danny?"

"You could eat him. He's sweet enough."

"I don't want to be around him."

"You ought to make up your mind."

"It's not like it was before. I hated him then. Now I see how cute he is, and understand why you're so crazy about him, and Jane is, and—why I was, for a little while. But I can't help it. I've got something in me. Every time I look at him I see Wash, and I can't forget what Wash did to me. I don't want to be around him."

"He's not Wash."

"I know it. I'm so ashamed."

"He's just a sweet, friendly little boy that's laughing at you all the time and sticking out his hand to touch

your face and showing you how good he can kick and
you ought to be thankful all day long that you've got
him."

"I ought to, but I'm not."

What she did about him was try to swallow down
how she felt, and play with him, and help Jane take care
of him, and drink. She told Jane it was Coca-Cola, but
all the time she was spiking it with the stuff we had
made, that was hidden all over the place, and when she
had a load of it she'd get a look in her eye, and I would
almost explode from wanting her. Every night she'd
slip down to me, and bring me some stuff, and we'd
drink it together, and there was no end to how much
we wanted each other. But Jane would get worried,
and go out looking for her, and once she almost caught
us, and that meant we had to do something. "Jess, we've
got to have a hide-out."

"Yeah, but where?"

"Have you forgotten our mine?"

Now the mine, after what I'd done with Moke, was
about the last place on earth I wanted to be. "I thought
we were done with all that stuff."

"What stuff? We don't have to run the still."

"It'll be there just the same."

"It doesn't have to be. I can take it down and put it
away if that's all that's bothering you. But it's secret.
It's like we used to say. Anything in the world could
be happening up there and nobody would ever know."

"You used to say it."

"And you used to think it."

She would borrow the truck after that and pretend
she was going to Carbon City for stuff that we needed,
and maybe she did go, I don't know. But one of those

times I had a look around, and found it parked in a place that could only mean she had gone up the mountain. And then one day she came out to where Jane and I were giving Danny his lunch with a basket on her arm. "Want to carry this for me, Jess, while I get some of those grapes up there in the woods, so we can have us some jelly?"

"You lost an arm or something?"

"It takes two hands for grapes."

"I never noticed it."

"First you got to find them, then you got to lift the vine up, where it hangs down over them, and then you got to cut the bunches off with a knife, so you don't mash them up trying to break them. And I want company. Wild grapes take a long time."

"Go along with her, Jess."

So we went, up the same old path, her a little ahead, humming a little, in between catching her breath. When we got to the timbered drift she went past it, then stopped.

"Would you like to see the little nook I've made in there?"

"Some other time, maybe."

"Not now? You sure?"

She half closed her eyes, and I don't know which was worse, the way my stomach was fluttering over Moke, or the way my heart was pounding over her.

"It'll only take a minute. Come on."

We went in, and got lamps out of the tool chest, and got as far as the entry where I'd buried Moke. "This old tunnel caved in since we were here, but that blocked the draft that used to blow through it, so of course that makes it a nice place to sit and pass the time."

In the tunnel mouth she had hung some candlewick

quilts like they sell on the way to town, and had fixed a seat. "But of course we can't have carbide, not romantic people like us."

Near the seat was a galvanized iron can we had used for water, with holes knocked in the bottom, and she held her lamp to one of them. It began to burn inside, and I saw it was half full of charcoal. "And with that good old Tyler corn and Coca-Cola, I thought we might cook ourselves something to eat."

She lifted the cover of the basket, and inside was a picked chicken. By then I wouldn't have left there if Moke had come right through the rock at me, so while she chased outside to grab some grapes quick, I went to the shaft mouth to grab some Coca-Cola we always kept in the spring water, and some corn. I was trembling so bad I never noticed that all the smell was gone, where she had emptied all that mash out, and put things in apple-pie order. I came back with the bottles, then went to the tool chest for a miner's needle, that I cleaned in the fire and ran through the chicken. I was almost done broiling it, trying not to think of her, when I jumped at the sound of music.

It was the radio, and she came in swinging her hips, and red fire shining up in her face, and looking right straight at me. That was one dance she never finished.

13

ONE MORNING, couple of months after that, there came a rap on the door and when I went out there it was Ed Blue. He wanted to know if I had seen anything of his rifle. I had my own rifle in reach, and after all that had happened I wouldn't have asked much to tell him to get the hell out and stay out or I'd plug him where he stood. But I thought I better see what he was up to. Because I knew where his rifle was all right. But at the same time I knew why he didn't have it. The way things were between him and Moke, Moke wouldn't have taken his rifle without him knowing it. And the way things were between me and Moke, Ed couldn't have helped knowing what Moke figured to do with it, even if Moke had said nothing about it, which wouldn't be like Moke. So when he began talking, I thought he was pretending rifle, but he really meant Moke. But after a while I saw that it was really his rifle he was after, and as well as I could tell, he had thought about it since Moke left him, and put it together something like this: Moke hadn't killed me, so something must have gone wrong with it. I hadn't killed Moke, or so far as he knew I hadn't, so what had happened? He probably said to himself, I'd run into Moke and maybe run him off the creek. But if I had I certainly wasn't letting Moke keep the gun. So why not come around, ask me about it, and watch my eyes?

I told him nothing, and he went off with a lot of talk about how he's a peaceable man, and sure would hate it if somebody got hurt by a gun that belonged to him, and by ganny he hopes he don't get sued. What anybody would get out of it if he did get sued he didn't say. But a couple of nights later, when the girls had gone to a picture show and taken Danny with them, and I had taken a walk by the creek to think things over and figure out where I was at with my life if I was anywhere at all, I started back to the cabin, and from down the road a ways I saw a light inside. I crept up on it, and there in the front room, shooting the light all around, was Ed. After he finished looking there he went on back and shot the light at the girl's clothes and under the bed. I waited till he was doing the same in the lean-to before I tiptoed inside, took my six-shooter down, and threw on him from the doorway of the front room.

"Put 'em up, Ed."

He had no gun, and he was reaching before he even turned around. I went over and took the light from him so it wouldn't burn down the house. "Now you goddam lop-eared cross-eyed good-for-nothing rat, for the last time what are you doing in my place and what do you want?"

"Jess, I'm only looking for my gun."

"You think I steal guns?"

"No—no, Jess, it ain't that. It's just that after what happened that day, when I done what Moke made me do at the funeral, I thought maybe you'd come up there and tooken it, just to be safe. That's all, I hope Christ may kill me."

"I didn't. You got that?"

"I got it, Jess."

"If I shot, you know, if I said a man was back there in my house and I shot him because I was afraid he would kill me, the law would uphold me. You know that?"

"I sure do know it, Jess."

"Suppose I let you go?"

"Anything you say, Jess."

"Cut out your snooping around."

I never said anything to her about it. I never said anything to her or anybody that would lead around to Moke. But it made me nervous. So of course she thought I was nervous on account of her, and that was how she liked it so she could laugh at me and sit in my lap and tickle my chin and say stop being so solemn. And then one day we were up there, behind the quilt that kind of cut us off from the timbered tunnel, and had had some drinks and stuff she had brought to eat, and the music was turned down soft, and she was dancing in front of me with not a stitch on. And then, from the other side of the quilt, I heard something no miner could ever mistake. It was the whisper that comes out of a carbide lamp when the flame has been cut but the water is still making gas.

I motioned her to keep on like she was, and hit the quilt with everything I had. Something went down, but so did the quilt, and it fell over the brazier, so the place went so black you couldn't see your hand. I hit, and landed. I hit again, and got one back in the jaw. I hit again, and just touched a shirt going away. Then there were steps, shuffling down the track. Then she screamed, and all of a sudden the place was full of light, where she had tried to get the quilt off the brazier, and red coals were all over, and the quilt was burning, and so were her clothes, where she had dropped them on the seat. When we put out the fire with water the place was full of steam. "Jess, who was it?"

"I don't know."

"What did they want?"

"I don't know."

"You think they saw anything?"

"I don't know that either."

But in my heart I knew it was Ed Blue, still snooping around after his rifle. And sure enough, next morning, when I was out back chopping apples for the cider press, Jane came out of the house and went running to a big tree on the other side of the barn, grabbed a boy that was hiding there, and slapped his face. When she came back she was white, the only time I ever saw her get mad. "The idea, talking like that!"

"What did he say to you?"

"It was to Kady. Calling her pappy-lover."

Kady came out, and listened, and didn't look at her or me. All morning I could hear Jane going on about it, but if Kady said anything I didn't hear it. Then in the afternoon she came to me, where I was up on the press turning it down, and said: "Jess, I'm going away."

"You're—what?"

"Going away. To Washington maybe. Some place."

"You mean you're leaving me?"

"I'm leaving you, and I'm taking Jane and Danny."

"But why?"

"You heard what happened this morning, and you saw how Jane carried on about it. I can't have any more of that. Maybe I've gone to hell, Jess, but I won't have her finding it out, and if she stays one more day on this creek she will. Somebody saw us, and somebody's spreading it."

"Maybe I won't let you go."

"I wasn't asking you."

"Maybe you forgot you're my wife."

"For God's sake, be your age."

I climbed down there to tell her the truth, but her eyes were just two slits in her face, and she looked cold. It came to me it wouldn't do any good to tell her. She wouldn't believe me, and there was no way in the world I could prove it.

"We're leaving today."

"You're in quite a hurry."

"I'm taking them away on the six o'clock bus out of Carbon City, and I'll thank you to drive us in there."

"Then all right."

Jane came to me just before we started, and she didn't have any idea what was going on, but she was unhappy about leaving me and tried to tell how much she thought of me. I felt that way too, and tried to figure some way I could keep on with Kady and square it up somehow with Jane. So I said maybe if I could sell the place I would go east myself, and she put her arms around me and said that would be wonderful. And whether I meant to take them to town I don't know, but I think I was going to have a breakdown on the state road, to stall it for one night, and in that time I might be able to think of something. But while we were still on the dirt road that runs beside the creek, we met a car coming up. It had two men in it, and when they saw us one of them raised his hand for me to stop.

"Are you Jess Tyler?"

"Who wants to know?"

"Sheriff's deputy."

He showed a badge and I said I wasn't saying who I was and if he wanted to know he had to find out some other way. "Well, there's a simple way to find out, Mr. Tyler. I just look at you and then I remember you from the time I made out papers on you once before. When you pretty near killed a man. Remember?"

"What do you want?"

"Serve a warrant for your arrest."

"What for?"

"Incest, this says."

"That's a lie."

"If it's a lie, then all you got to do is prove it to the court. My job is to serve papers. Is this your daughter Kady?"

"I told you, find out for yourself."

"Miss Tyler, I remember you too, and I have a court order here for your detention as a material witness. Now then, how shall we do about the truck? Mr. Tyler, do you want me to drive in to Carbon with you, or would you and your daughters prefer to ride with the other deputy while I take your truck wherever you want it or have you got some idea of your own?"

"My other daughter will drive it."

"Then we're set."

Kady and I got out and got in the other car and neither of us said anything to Jane at all. But out of the corner of my eye I could see her sitting there in the sun, the baby on her lap, staring at us.

14

When the deputy brought me to court, Jane was waiting, with Danny on her shoulder, trying to keep him quiet where he was crying because it was away past his bedtime. A whole bunch of people were there, because the Carbon City radio had put out about the arrest on the seven o'clock broadcast, and half the people in town came running over to the courthouse for the hearing. My case hadn't been called yet, and while I was standing in the hall with the deputy, Jane came running over. "How could you do this to her, Jess?"

The deputy cut in to remind her that anything that was said could be used against me, but she didn't pay any attention to him.

"You knew all along what it had done to her, Wash walking out like he did. You knew she was drinking. You knew she wasn't herself, that she'd do almost anything that anybody told her to. And yet you would take advantage of her in the way you did."

"You sure I did?"

"If you didn't, wouldn't she tell me? She don't lie to me. If she won't look at me and won't say anything to me, that means you did just what they say you did."

"There might be more to it than that."

The jail warden's wife came in about that time with Kady, and Jane left me and went over to her. A minute or two later Ed Blue came in, with every man, woman, and child from Tulip, and I knew what I was in for.

It was the same old judge and he watched us line up and asked the deputies a few things, like did I have a lawyer, and kept looking at me like I was some kind of a toad frog he was afraid would give him warts if he wasn't careful. Then he began talking to me: "Jess Tyler, you stand before me accused of the crime of incest, consisting of sexual misconduct with your daughter, Kady Tyler, and of corrupting the morals of a minor, Kady Tyler. How do you plead?"

"What's plead?"

"You plead when you enter a plea, declaring yourself guilty or not guilty. If you plead guilty, it will be my duty to set bail, and pending its deposit, to hold you for sentence by the circuit court. If you plead not guilty, or elect not to plead at this hearing, as you have the right to do, it will be my duty to hear the evidence against you, and if in my judgment, it is competent, material, and substantial, to hold you for action by the grand jury, set bail, and pending its deposit, to turn you over to the custody of the sheriff."

"And what do you do to her?"

"Your daughter is not under charges."

"She's arrested just the same."

"As a material witness, entitled to bail."

"What I'm getting at, it looks to me like if I plead guilty and you hold me, then you wouldn't need a witness any more and she could go home. But I'm not doing it without I make sure."

"Mr. Prosecutor?"

A young fellow standing with Ed Blue spoke up and said: "Your honor, the only charge made against this girl was a complaint sworn out by the sheriff's office which charges her with indecent exposure, but as it describes an act not committed in a public place it sets up no violation of the statute and I am accordingly quashing it. Otherwise, unless evidence not now known to me comes to light, if this man chooses to save the state the expense of a trial and avoid further scandal, he's quite right. On his plea of guilty I won't need the witness, and while the higher court may want to question her before passing sentence, I wouldn't ask this court to require bail. To clear up our general attitude in cases of this kind, though not in any way binding myself or entering into a bargain of any kind, we rarely ask commitment to reform school, or penological steps of any kind, for a girl who is at the same time the mother of a young child, unless circumstances exist which compel us to. Does that answer you, Tyler?"

"I plead guilty."

"Then I set bail at five thousand dollars pending sentence. Are you prepared to furnish it tonight?"

"No sir, I'm not."

"Take him to jail. Next case."

The next case was a colored fellow that had been arrested for stealing a tire, and he was on the front bench of the courtroom, and stood up with a deputy. My deputy started off with me, but I heard the judge tell somebody to stand aside, and when I looked around Kady was still standing there. And then all of a sudden she looked up, stared the judge straight in the eye, and said: "He's not guilty of anything."

"Your father has already pleaded."

"My husband, you mean."

"*What?*"

"We got married."

"Officer, bring that man back."

The prosecutor, that had seemed like a nice young fellow, turned into a wolf, and he took at least an hour, snapping question after question at her, until he had it all, how we had gone to Gilroy that day and said in the marriage license bureau we had the same name but were no relation, that her father's name was Hiram Tyler and he was dead, and that she was twenty-two years old. The judge cut in with a lot of stuff he wanted to know about, and after a while the prosecutor said: "Your honor, this is as shocking a thing as I've encountered in all my experience at the bar. Occasional morals cases come up, but this is the first time I ever heard of where two people went before an officer of this state and deliberately made a mockery of it and its laws. I don't know where it leads to, but the very least I can ask of this court is to hold this girl for the action of the grand jury."

"So ordered."

She had plenty of back talk, and said I had done what I had done because I loved her, and things were due to happen between us anyway, and I wanted it in wedlock, like it should be, and didn't know it was against the law. Where she got was nowhere. The judge tore into her and the prosecutor did, but all the time I was thinking of what they would do to her for perjury, and how at last I had to tell the truth, even if she hated me for it and I never saw her again. "I'm changing that plea."

"And how about your new plea?"

"What new plea, your honor?"

"To the new charge, perjury."

"My plea to that charge and both the other charges is not guilty. This girl is not my daughter, but she is my wife, and what law we've been violating I'd like somebody to explain me."

"What do you mean she's not your daughter?"

"I mean what I say."

"Whose daughter is she then?"

"Man by the name of Moke Blue."

"That's a lie!"

It snapped out of her before she even knew she was going to say it, and right away she apologized for it.

"I'm sorry, Jess, to use that word. I take it back, but you'll have to take back what you said too. Even if it's to save me I can't bear to hear that."

"It's not a lie and I don't take it back."

"Who's Moke Blue?"

I told them who Moke was, how he had broken up my home, how he and Belle had gone off together, how it had all started about a year before Kady was born. I didn't have any of it learned by heart or anything. I didn't even know what I was going to say next. "And you knew Moke Blue was her father?"

"I knew I wasn't."

"But you raised her just the same?"

"I never saw her from the day my wife took her away with her till a year ago when she came with me to live."

"And you started sleeping with her?"

"I did not."

"When did you start?"

"After we were married."

"You lived with her all that time in the same house and did nothing to her at all and then all of a sudden you decided it was time to marry her. Why didn't you marry her before?"

"I was already married."

"So we've got a little bigamy here too?"

"My wife, my first wife, this wife's mother, died. The day after that I asked Kady to marry me. She said all right and we went to Gilroy."

"You had her misrepresent her age?"

"I'd forgotten her age."

"And misrepresent the name of her father?"

"After we were married, when she told me she had put down her father's name as Hiram Tyler, was the first I knew she really thought I was her father. I thought she knew about Moke."

"Didn't you tell her?"

"Then? I tried to, but I couldn't."

"Why not?"

"You heard her just now. Moke was a shiftless, no-account nothing, and if I told her the truth about him I thought she'd hate me for it and I loved her and didn't want her to."

"Where is this Moke Blue?"

"I don't know."

The judge and the prosecutor looked at each other, and then the judge said to Kady: "Young woman, do you believe any of this?"

She didn't answer, and he asked who Jane was and asked the same thing of her. She didn't answer, either. "Is there any neighbor of this man, who knew him and his wife at the time they were living together, who will testify he believes it, or had any knowledge of it at the time?"

Nobody said anything. I said Moke had the same butterfly on his stomach that Danny had, that only the men in his family were born with it, and that Kady didn't have it but the boy did, and they didn't even bother to wake Danny up to look, where he was stretched out on the desk, with Jane's hat over his eyes to keep the light out. I was sunk, and I knew it, and Kady was sunk, and I knew that too. Until, all of a sudden, I happened to look at Ed Blue, and the look on his face told me I wasn't sunk, that I was going to win, that I'd rip it right out of him, what I had to have to be turned loose. The judge got ready to wind up the case. "Well, Tyler, until you get Moke Blue in court and produce some sort of direct substantiation of what you say, I'm afraid I'll have to regard it as a far-fetched invention to escape the consequences of several serious crimes, so—"

"I can't get him up here."

"Why not?"

"He's afraid to come."

"What's he afraid of?"

"That I'll kill him."

"Why would he be afraid of that?"

He was looking at me like I was making a fool of myself and didn't know it but he would give me all the chance I wanted, and that was just how I wanted him to feel. "Because I ordered him off the creek when he tried to kill me, with a rifle that was lent him to do it with by this lying rat that's come in here to testify against me, that's his half brother *and that has the same butterfly on his stomach this child has and that he's not*

*saying anything about because he wants me sent up for
something I didn't do!"*

If you think that don't set off a bombshell in that
courtroom, you don't know what a judge feels like
when he thinks somebody has been trying to put something over on him. He was so sore I thought he'd hit
Ed. He had him take off his shirt, and unbuttoned
Danny's little suit himself, so gentle it was like he was
his own son. And on Ed, sure enough, was the butterfly,
all fixed up with curlicue feelers and red border, from
the time he fired on the railroad and a tattoo man in
Norfolk had fixed him up, or so he told the court.

"And this half brother of yours, this Moke Blue, has
this butterfly too?"

"I don't know, sir."

"Do you want to be charged with perjury too?"

"Yes sir, he has it."

"And only the men in your family have it?"

"I heard so."

The judge drummed on the desk with his fingers, then
leaned over and whispered with the prosecutor. Then:
"Tyler, in the light of this piece of evidence, I'm not
at all sure that I'm convinced of your innocence. Mor-
ally, it seems to me there was something queer about
your failure to tell this girl of her parentage, and let
her go on thinking she was guilty of something that
must have struck her as utterly loathsome. But I am
convinced that if these birthmarks are shown to a jury,
whether Moke Blue can be located or not, it is going to
be impossible to get them to convict you. So I'm dis-
missing the charge. But God help you if you're in trouble, on the basis of new evidence, in connection with
this case again."

"I won't be. I'm not guilty."

"That reminds me: Why did you enter your plea of guilty in the first place? That still seems a queer thing to do."

"I told you, I didn't want her to know."

"About Moke Blue being her father?"

"That's it."

"You must indeed be in love with her."

"I might be."

15

FOR THE NEXT WEEK she hardly looked at me, and stayed on in the back room, while I stayed on at the stable. But she kept studying Danny and the butterfly, and you could tell she was trying to get used to it, what it meant. And then one day before the fire, while Jane was out back cooking supper, she picked him up in her arms, and said: "My little boy." She said it over and over, with tears shining in her eyes and running down her face. After that she began taking care of him, and wouldn't let Jane do anything at all. Then was when she began to notice me again, and watch me, like she was studying about something. And then one morning, just before daylight, she came down to the stable with a lantern, and I had a wild idea she had come to make up and be my wife. But she wasn't thinking of that, even a little bit. She hadn't undressed from the night before, and set the lantern down, and sat on my bunk with it shining up on her face, so I could see it but couldn't see her eyes. "Jess, ever since that night in the courtroom, I've been thinking back, trying to remember how it all was, and specially that's what I've been doing tonight. And there's one thing I've got to know."

"I'll tell you anything I can."

"When did you first know Moke was my father?"

"Before you were born, even."

"And how did you know?"

"I knew I wasn't."

"You mean there had been nothing between you and Belle for some time and that meant somebody else had to be my father and you figured it had to be Moke?"

"That's it."

"Why didn't he tell me?"

"Maybe Belle wouldn't let him."

"What reason could she have for not letting him?"

"Ashamed, maybe."

"Or maybe she didn't know it."

"If I knew it, she had to."

"Not if only the men in that family had the butterfly. I haven't got it. Maybe neither of them knew it until Danny came and they saw the birthmark. Maybe that's why they began to fight. Maybe that's why Moke took Danny. Maybe that's why Belle tried to kill him, to keep him from saying anything to me about it."

"I tell you, if I knew it—"

"Jess, there's a simple answer to that."

"What is it?"

"You might be lying to me. Right now. About knowing it before I was born, about how it was between you and Belle then, and all the rest of it."

"I might be an Indian, but I'm not."

She stretched out on top of the blankets and stared

up at the harness that was hanging on pegs over our heads, and it was quite a while before she said anything. "Jess, you *are* lying."

"If you think so, all right."

"You didn't know it when we were up there in the mine every day, running liquor, and in town every night, selling it."

"What makes you think I didn't?"

"The passes I was making."

"I fought you off."

"But why?"

"Didn't you hear me in court? I was married."

"Jess, don't make me laugh."

"That's funny to you, being married?"

"Jess, the way you wanted me, being married wouldn't have meant any more to you than nothing. And what are you trying to tell me? You hadn't seen Belle for eighteen years, and just because you hadn't taken the trouble to get a divorce, and she hadn't, you think I'm going to believe it you were still worrying about being married? But laying up with your own daughter, that would be something else. That would be something you would think you had to fight. That would mean plenty to you on Sunday, when you were going to church and singing the hymns and worrying about hell-fire after you die. Jess, why don't you own up to it? At that time you thought I was your daughter."

"I own up to nothing."

It began to get light, and still she lay there, and after a while she said: "And you didn't know I wasn't your daughter that day Belle was dying."

"You seem to have it all figured out."

"That detective work you were doing, about why

she tried to do something to Moke. If you knew about this, why couldn't you figure that out? But you never once thought of it."

"I told you, I thought you already knew it, only you hadn't said anything to me about it. Later, when I found out you didn't know it, then I began to get it, why she went out of her head so, on that trip up here."

"And you didn't know it my wedding day!"

"Our wedding day."

"Our wedding day, my eye. I've only had one wedding day, and it wasn't ours. But you, you're lying to me if you say you knew it that morning. You weren't married any more, and yet you were willing I should marry Wash, and glad of it. For your daughter, that makes sense. But for Moke's daughter? A girl that was no relation to you at all, and that you wanted so bad you couldn't sleep nights? Oh no, Jess. That day was the day you found it out. I thought then there was some connection between the way you disappeared and Wash not showing up, and now God help me I have the same feeling."

"No connection I know of."

"And Moke hasn't been seen since that day. Maybe there's some connection there too. If you saw him, why didn't you tell me?"

"I wanted to forget Moke."

"Why didn't you tell Ed Blue?"

"I still wanted to forget him."

"Seems funny you didn't snap it into Ed Blue's face about the rifle and how you warned Moke off the creek, like you told the judge."

"Let him look for his rifle."

"Where is the rifle?"

"I threw it in the creek."

"Where's Moke?"

"How should I know?"

"Jess, you killed Moke, didn't you?"

The prickle up my back had told me what she was going to say, but for once my mouth went off and left me. I said something. I hollered no, but it was after at least three seconds of trying to act surprised, like I didn't know what she was talking about. She was already laughing at me not being able to make up my mind when this croak came out of my throat, a cold, hard laugh that had my number, and knew it.

When I went in for breakfast, it was she that gave it to me. When Jane came in she was dressed to go out, with her hat on, and a coat.

"Well, Jess, I'll say good-by."

"Where you going?"

"Blount, I guess."

"You mean you're leaving me?"

"I'm not really needed any more, now that Kady takes care of Danny so well, and there's a fellow over there that's offered me a job in his café, helping him run it. It's time I took him up."

"Kind of sudden, isn't it?"

"Oh I've been thinking about it."

But she said it all in a queer way, fooling with her bag while she talked, and it seemed to me she was going for some special reason she wasn't telling me. "Then I'll run you over there."

"I'm taking the bus."

"I'll run you to the state road."

"I can walk."

"You need any money?"

"I've got some."

On account of waking up early I felt tired that afternoon, and how long I slept I don't know, but Kady was standing there when I woke up, all dressed up, looking at me. "Good-by, Jess."

"And where are *you* going?"

"To be married."

"When?"

"Next week some time."

"You *are* married. Did you forget that?"

"No, I didn't."

"Then how can you get married?"

"Next week I'll be able to."

"That I don't understand."

"You will."

"And who's the lucky man?"

"Wash."

"Changed his mind again, hey?"

"He found out the truth, at last. Jane called him when she got to Blount. In fact, that might be partly why she went over there."

"I knew she wasn't telling me the reason."

"She called him and he came in and was crazy to know what had happened up here, because it was on the radio when you were arrested but not in the papers when they turned you loose, because if nobody gets convicted they're afraid. So she told him what you told the judge, and he ran her back over here again. Jess, you told him Moke was Danny's father. You told me he was *my* father. And both were lies. You're my father. But you don't tell any third lie. You got that,

Jess? You understand why next week I can get married?"

"You'll get into plenty trouble that way."

"We don't think so."

"I tell you, the deputies will find it out, sure."

"We're going to tell them."

It seemed funny, she was never going to believe the truth, and I had killed the one man that could prove it. And when they heard what she thought was the truth, no jury would hold her for what she meant to do to me.

Outside it had started to rain, and when I peeped through a crack she was running down the road to his car, that had the top up, and inside I could see Jane and the baby. She got in and the car drove off. I went to the cabin for my rifle. It wasn't there, and neither was the .45. I put on my hat and coat and started down to the barn, to get out the truck and run into Carbon to get sheriff's protection. But when I got to the door a shot cut the air, and splinters ripped off the wood. I started back to the house, and another shot clipped my hat. I slammed down on my face, and when it got darker I crawled. Out in the stable I could hear the stock bellowing, and down the creek the cows were hooking it up, but I was afraid to go outside. Later on, after I had made myself something to eat without stirring up the fire, for fear they were looking through the cracks and could see, I got all my money together and put on my raincoat and started creeping down the road. All over, you could hear bellowing from pigs and mules and chickens and cows that hadn't been fed or milked or attended to. I got about two hundred yards when something hit my leg and I heard a shot. I crawled back, doused it with liniment, and got the blood stopped.

It's been raining for a week, they've been out there for a week, and I've been writing for a week. Maybe they've got to kill me to wipe it all out, what happened, so they can have each other again, or think they have, and maybe they're going to tell it, so they get off. But I've got to tell it too, because I didn't do anything but what I thought was right. What I told him I thought was true, and if he didn't think enough of her to go see her about it, to give her her chance to say what she had to say, then that was his lookout. After I found out how it really was, she was anybody's woman, and all I've got to say is, I love her as much as he does. So I'm putting it down. It's finished now, and tonight I'm taking it with me when I leave, and maybe there won't have to be any telling, and they'll decide they can have each other without any killing. Because my leg's better now, and there's one thing they've forgotten. And that's the mine.

I slipped out the back way when it got dark, crossed the creek above the cabin, and got up the path without their seeing me. I got to the timbered drift, went inside, and soon as I was well inside so no light could be seen from the road I got out the carbide lamp I had brought with me. All I had to do now was slip through to the bottom of the shaft, go up the ladder to the top, kill the light, and then slide down the mountainside and come out on the road about a mile below where they're laying for me. From there on to the bus stop is a short walk, and I'd be away. But when I hit the lamp to strike the flint, I dropped it, and I heard the top pop open and the carbide go all over the track. And while I was feeling around for a couple of crumbs I could put in there with a little spit, I heard something that almost made me drop dead. It was Moke, in there under the tunnel, prizing around with the gun barrel, trying to get out. He would hit a rock three or four times, then get the steel in a crack, twist it around, move a chunk, then start all over again. I gave a yell and started to run out of the place, but I fell and hit my head and that was the last I knew for a while. When I came to he was nearer, and I could hear his chinking plainer. I got out of there somehow. When I got back here it was day.

It's still raining out, but it's daylight now, and I've been listening to the water run off the roof and I've figured out what that was in the mine. It wasn't Moke. It was water dripping. Now I know what it is, I won't mind it any more, and tonight I'll get out of here.

I'm cut off. Ed Blue is out there and

ABOUT THE AUTHOR

JAMES M. CAIN (1892–1977) is recognized today as one of the masters of the hard-boiled school of American novels. Born in Baltimore, the son of the president of Washington College, he began his career as reporter on the Baltimore papers, served in the American Expeditionary Force in World War I and wrote the material for *The Cross of Lorraine*, the newspaper of the 79th Division. He returned to become professor of journalism at St. John's College in Annapolis and then worked for H. L. Mencken on *The American Mercury*. He later wrote editorials for Walter Lippmann on the *New York World* and was for a short period managing editor of *The New Yorker*, before he went to Hollywood as a script writer. His first novel, *The Postman Always Rings Twice*, was published when he was forty-two and at once became a sensation. It was tried for obscenity in Boston, was said by Albert Camus to have inspired his own book, *The Stranger*, and is now a classic. Cain followed it the next year with *Double Indemnity*, leading Ross Macdonald to write years later, "Cain has won unfading laurels with a pair of native American masterpieces, *Postman* and *Double Indemnity*, back to back." Cain published eighteen books in all and was working on his autobiography at the time of his death.

VINTAGE MYSTERIES

V-53	**BOX, EDGAR** / Death Before Bedtime
V-54	**BOX, EDGAR** / Death In the Fifth Position
V-55	**BOX, EDGAR** / Death Likes It Hot
V-212	**CAIN, JAMES M.** / The Butterfly
V-581	**CAIN, JAMES M.** / Double Indemnity
V-213	**CAIN, JAMES M.** / Love's Lovely Counterfeit
V-582	**CAIN, JAMES M.** / Mildred Pierce
V-583	**CAIN, JAMES M.** / The Postman Always Rings Twice
V-585	**CAIN, JAMES M.** / Serenade
V-631	**CHANDLER, RAYMOND** / The Big Sleep
V-138	**CHANDLER, RAYMOND** / Farewell, My Lovely
V-141	**CHANDLER, RAYMOND** / The High Window
V-145	**CHANDLER, RAYMOND** / The Lady In The Lake
V-550	**FREELING, NICOLAS** / Auprès De Ma Blonde
V-551	**FREELING, NICOLAS** / The Bugles Blowing
V-552	**FREELING, NICOLAS** / The Night Lords
V-553	**FREELING, NICOLAS** / Sabina
V-829	**HAMMETT, DASHIELL** / The Big Knockover
V-2013	**HAMMETT, DASHIELL** / The Continental Op
V-624	**HAMMETT, DASHIELL** / The Dain Curse
V-773	**HAMMETT, DASHIELL** / The Glass Key
V-772	**HAMMETT, DASHIELL** / The Maltese Falcon
V-828	**HAMMETT, DASHIELL** / Red Harvest
V-774	**HAMMETT, DASHIELL** / The Thin Man
V-648	**ROUGHEAD, WILLIAM** / Classic Crimes
V-309	**RUHM, HERBERT (ed.)** / The Hard-Boiled Detective
V-274	**WAHLÖO, PER AND MAJ SJÖWALL** / The Abominable Man
V-444	**WAHLÖO, PER AND MAJ SJÖWALL** / Cop Killer
V-340	**WAHLÖO, PER AND MAJ SJÖWALL** / The Fire Engine That Disappeared
V-341	**WAHLÖO, PER AND MAJ SJÖWALL** / The Laughing Policeman
V-274	**WAHLÖO, PER AND MAJ SJÖWALL** / The Locked Room
V-777	**WAHLÖO, PER AND MAJ SJÖWALL** / The Man On The Balcony
V-778	**WAHLÖO, PER AND MAJ SJÖWALL** / The Man Who Went Up In Smoke
V-342	**WAHLÖO, PER AND MAJ SJÖWALL** / Murder At The Savoy
V-779	**WAHLÖO, PER AND MAJ SJÖWALL** / Roseanna
V-452	**WAHLÖO, PER AND MAJ SJÖWALL** / The Terrorists